# Survival Skills

# Survival Skills

*Stories by*
**Jean Ryan**

Ashland
Creek
Press

*Survival Skills*

Stories by Jean Ryan

Published by Ashland Creek Press

www.ashlandcreekpress.com

ISBN 978-1-61822-021-9

Library of Congress Control Number: 2012938514

Printed in the United States of America on acid-free paper. All paper products used to create this book are Sustainable Forestry Initiative (SFI) Certified Sourcing.

Cover and book design by John Yunker.

For Cindy,

with gratitude and boundless admiration

# Contents

# Greyhound

This place is not like the pound—greyhounds don't bark, nor do they make any frenetic appeals for freedom, nor do their sleek bodies betray any sign of disease. Professional athletes, these dogs have been fed and watered with precision. Now, finally pardoned, they rest comfortably in their cages, and as I approach, they raise their heads and eye me warily: What am I doing here? What do I want from them?

Pick one, I keep telling myself. But how? They look away, refuse to help me.

"Do you know anything about them?" I ask the attendant, a plump blonde in a tight green uniform. "Their personalities, I mean."

"Sure." She pushes herself off the wall and points to the dog in front of us. "That's Digger Dan. He's five. Raced in eight states. He's stubborn but real smart. And that's Buck Shot. He's four, kind of skittery."

We move down the row. "Shoot the Moon's a good dog." She shrugs. "They're all good dogs." We stop at another cage and peer at a brindled greyhound the colors of a fawn. "This one's new." The blonde puts her hands on her hips and chuckles. "You know what she did? She stopped running. The gate opened one day, and she wouldn't budge."

She is lying still as a sphinx, paws neatly crossed, tail tucked away. Her deep brown eyes appraise us; there's no telling what she concludes. I stare back, and her gaze slides off.

"How old is she?" I ask.

"Three. She ran for just over a year. Clara's Gift, they called her. She was good, a favorite. Funny the way she quit."

The dog is waiting for us to leave—I can see the tension in the sculpted muscles of her back.

I wonder if, tired of racing, she planned her defection. How long did it take her to get up the nerve? Did she know when they led her to the track that day?

Or maybe the idea came to her suddenly. Maybe, as she crouched behind the gate, as the crowd filled the bleachers, she added the whole thing up and saw at long last that she was being duped: The rabbit wasn't real.

"Can I pet her?" I ask.

"They're not used to affection," the blonde says, opening the cage. "They don't understand it."

I come closer, and the dog rises to a sitting position. Her eyes are large and apprehensive. Carefully I extend my hand; she sniffs it and shrinks. When I touch her, she flinches. "Good girl," I soothe, and though she allows me to pet her shoulder, it's not much fun for either of us.

Great. I could have gone to the pound and come back thirty minutes later with a fat, tail-wagging puppy, but here I am at the greyhound shelter, 112 miles from home, offering up my heart to a dog who just wishes I'd go away.

I arch an eyebrow at the attendant, and she smiles sympathetically.

"They're all like that in the beginning," she assures me, "and then, after a few weeks, they can't get enough of it." Dubious, I turn back to the dog, who is looking at my arm as if it were a rolled-up newspaper.

"Just move slowly," she says. "They don't like sudden movements. And they don't like having their crate space invaded."

"Crate space?"

She nods. "Greyhounds spend most of their time in crates—they sleep in them; they feel safe in them. These cages are like their crates."

I pull my arm out, and the dog cautiously lowers herself back down. There is no waste on this animal; she is muscle and tendon, angle and bone; even her veins have no place to hide. Her forelegs are so thin and straight I have to turn away. There must be thirty dogs here, all posed in their cages, remote and silent as statuary.

"I thought they'd be old," I say.

"Oh, no. Two years of racing is about the norm. Some of them run longer—you can tell by their paws." She points to a large black-and-white hound. "Like that one. See how his front toes are twisted? The oval track does that. Most of these dogs are retired because of injury, or because they stop winning."

"Or running," I add, bringing my gaze back to Clara's Gift, realizing I have made my choice. And she knows, too, even before I tell the attendant. Alarmed, she gets to her feet, prepares to submit. It breaks my heart how good she is about being taken away, how dignified her walk to my truck. What price has she paid to behave like that?

Figuring she might enjoy some scenery for a change, I let her ride in the cab. She perches on the bench seat, taking up almost no space, and looks worriedly out the window. I keep murmuring assurances, but my voice doesn't calm her. As soon as we merge onto the highway and the Oregon mountains begin rushing by, she crawls off the seat and into the back of the cab.

~

The dog is a present for Holly, a surprise. She thinks I'm running errands for the store, picking up organic lettuces and local honey. That's where we met, my health food store. She came in one day and showed me the patches of eczema on her arms and asked me what she could do about them. I told her she might try using a humidifier, and I sold her some B-complex vitamins and a bar of oatmeal soap. Not long after that she moved in with me, and six years later we're still together, and still battling that eczema.

Not every day, of course—it comes and goes like magic. For weeks, even months, her limbs are as smooth and pale as the creamy hollows of a seashell. Most of the bouts are mild—mainly on her arms and the back of her hands—but there are times when the rash terrifies us both, when it moves up her neck and down her chest, turning the skin into a silvery crust, till she hides herself even from me. Those are the times she can't sleep, and I find her on the back steps rocking herself in the moonlight.

This has been a tough year for Holly—four episodes already— and two weeks ago, at the start of another flare-up, she quit her job at the Talking Turtle Day Care Center. The parents were making comments, she told me. "They get edgy at the sight of a rash, especially on an adult."

"What about the children?" I asked. "What do they say?"

"Oh, they don't mind. They just want to know if it hurts."

I have persuaded her to take at least six months off, hoping some private time will hush her demons (of course I don't mention this, for fear of jinxing her). I must admit I like the idea of her at home, making cheese lasagna and repotting plants. Still, it's a shame about the day care center: Nobody's better with children than Holly. She can remember their world, can still lose herself gazing at a puddle of tadpoles. She is childlike even in appearance, with her thin limbs and small, sharp features. People can't believe she is thirty-nine years old.

A dog, I thought, would be a good idea, would satisfy Holly's nurturing needs while presenting fewer challenges than a roomful of children bored with their toys. So when I saw the ad for adopting a retired greyhound, I couldn't ignore the serendipity.

~

Now, halfway home, glancing at the pile of literature they gave me, I'm having second thoughts. Greyhounds come with a list of warnings: Did I know they shouldn't be left alone? Is my neighborhood quiet? Any toddlers in the house? And is there a fenced-in field nearby? Once these dogs start running, God knows where they'll end up.

All I can see of Clara's Gift are her front paws; she hasn't moved in over an hour, hasn't offered so much as a sigh. I don't expect her to jump around joyfully, but why, on the other hand, doesn't she whimper? For all she knows, we could be heading for another racetrack.

I think of her sticklike limbs; they remind me of invalids, of nursing homes and wheelchairs. Suddenly I don't think I can do this. I am a large woman, big-boned—you wouldn't guess, looking at Holly and me, that I'm the squeamish one. Truth is, I can't stomach the suffering of animals; I can't even walk into a pet store. An exit sign appears, and I move into the right lane. Would it be so unforgivable, bringing back this damaged dog?

But I don't. I take her home to Holly, as I do the fallen fledglings

I find, and all the other hapless creatures I don't know how to fix.

~

"She needs a special diet. And we have to walk her twice a day." I'm citing the drawbacks right away, letting Holly know what we're up against. "And, ah, she isn't housebroken either—none of them are."

But Holly is scarcely listening. Sitting on her heels, facing the dog, she is already smitten.

"She's so delicate," Holly says. "Like a deer, or like one of those tiny primeval horses."

"We'll have to run her in the soccer field, a couple times a week," I add. "Greyhounds need to run."

"What did you say they called her?"

"Clara's Gift."

"What kind of a name is that?" Holly shakes her head. "No. We'll call her"—she pauses, smiles—"we'll call her Fawn." At the utterance of this word, soft and perfect, the dog lifts her small folded ears.

~

Shortly after arriving, Fawn wedges herself behind the sofa. "The room is too big," I explain to Holly. We find a cardboard carton in the garage, and Holly covers the bottom of it with an afghan her mother crocheted. We place the box next to the sofa, and, quick as a card trick, Fawn is inside.

~

For the next few days Fawn spends most of her time in that makeshift crate, calmly watching us drink our coffee, read the mail, open and close the drapes. At night, though, when Holly and I are in bed, I sometimes see her dark silhouette in the doorway. "Come here, Fawn," I coax, "come here, girl." But she declines the invitation, and after a while I hear her nails clicking down the hall as she makes her way back to her box. Whatever she needs, it's not our company.

As far as upkeep, she's no trouble at all. In fact, she's already housebroken. All I did was lay down some newspaper in a corner, and each morning I moved the papers a little closer to the back porch, and by the third day she was waiting at the door. There is something uncanny about this dog, some kind of age-old wisdom behind those luminous eyes. I get the feeling she is smarter than me and obeys out of politeness. Not that I need to issue many commands; Fawn comports herself so flawlessly I am embarrassed to put her on a leash. They told me to hold her firmly, that the twitch of a squirrel's tail would make her bolt. Well, we've seen plenty of squirrels, and even a few jackrabbits zigzagging through the scrub oak, and Fawn ignores them all. We've tried everything, from throwing sticks and Frisbees to jogging way ahead of her, and the thing is, she just won't run.

~

I am sitting on the sofa studying vitamin catalogs. Holly is lying on the carpet next to Fawn; over and over, her hand moves down the smooth slope of the dog's neck. Fawn no longer needs the box, and while she doesn't exactly ask for affection, she doesn't object to it either (unless you try to hug her—she can't bear that).

I spend too much time on these catalogs. They used to be newsprint pamphlets; today they're slick with photos, hefty as phone books. When I opened Earthly Goods eighteen years ago, there wasn't a pill in the place, just brown rice and bulgur and some bug-ravaged produce. I liked it that way; I liked the weirdly shaped tomatoes and the warm hayloft smell when I opened the door each morning. Now

I'm buying amino wafers and colloidal silver, royal jelly and blue-green algae. I had to cut back on the produce to make room for the bodybuilding products. Half of the back wall is devoted to nothing but B vitamins. I want to reduce my inventory, but everything sells: grape-seed extract, lutein, selenium, milk thistle, bovine cartilage. People are frantic for elixirs, and I'm the town supplier. I'm not even culpable when the potions don't work: The fault could lie in the alignment of the stars, in the user's lack of faith. That's the key to this booming business—the disclaimer's built right in.

I push aside the catalogs and consider the raw patches of skin on Holly's arms. Certainly nothing on my shelves has worked any miracles here. I wonder why the rash is so persistent this time and how bad it will get. Holly claims she has no secrets, no private well of grief; I can't believe this. I want to ask all the old questions, one by one, to see if there's something we've missed.

"Such soft fur," Holly says, her hand moving slowly, reverently down the dog's back. "They used to have wiry coats, like Airedales, but that's been bred out of them." Holly has been reading everything she can find on the subject of greyhounds. "Their eyes weren't this big either—the breeders decided that big eyes would make them see the lure better, so they elongated the head and made the occipital cavities larger—the sense of smell was impaired in the process, but nobody cared about that."

She sighs. "They even changed the tails, made them longer so they could work like rudders. The only trouble is, they keep breaking. Puppies break their tails all the time. Their legs break, too, especially the Italian greyhounds."

I think of the times I've seen Fawn gingerly lick her legs, or stare at them in a kind of bewilderment. At first we thought she might be in pain, which would explain her reluctance to run, but the vet said no, she was fine. "She's still a young dog," he said. "You really should run her—otherwise she'll get fat, and then she really will have problems."

Fawn's gaze is fixed on the carpet. Greyhounds originated in Egypt, Holly told me, and were called "gazehounds." I observe Fawn's glistening brown eyes, their dark depths keeping the secrets of the pharaohs. How can we make it up to her? How can we explain this powder-blue carpet to an animal that once roamed the banks of the Nile?

"I've never seen her wag her tail," I say. "Have you?"

"No," Holly says softly. She raises her hand and cups the small blameless dome of Fawn's head; the dog responds with a look of forbearance in which I can glimpse the burgeoning of devotion.

"Fawn has never been alone," Holly says. "She's lived her whole life with other dogs. Maybe we should let her spend some time with Maxine and Crash."

We share a nervous glance. Maxine and Crash live next door. Maxine is an old one-eyed mastiff; overweight, hobbled by arthritis, she still hauls herself over to the fence at the slightest provocation. Crash is a two-year-old black lab who in endless ebullience hurls his body into whatever objects lie in his path. Neither one is very bright, and they both bark too much, a habit we don't want Fawn to pick up.

"We could try it," Holly says. "We could take her over there and see how it goes."

I am weighing alternatives. There is a Chihuahua down the road who can teach Fawn nothing I want her to learn. Frank and Dora's Dalmatian would be more suitable, but they live four miles away; we'd have to drive there every time, and I really don't like Frank.

"Okay," I finally answer.

Fawn is studying the carpet again. I am sending my autistic child off to public school.

~

We have two rocks in our living room, boulders really; Holly rolled them in from the woods. There is a cavity in one, which she keeps filled with water; she's planted some emerald moss around it and a few tiny ferns. Miniature worlds—that's her fetish. Right now, she's working on a desert scene: a shallow clay bowl filled with sand to which she has introduced some baby cacti, a twig painted like a snake, an Ivory soap steer skull the size of a cough drop, and a prospector's shack she fashioned out of splinters from our fence. Last night she was talking about turning the hallway into a prehistoric diorama.

Holly went to art school back east and after graduation found herself on Fifth Avenue designing window displays. The winter scenes were the most fun, she said: the pumpkins and fall leaves, the sparkling drifts of plastic snow. Still, she got tired of the gaunt mannequins and the New York winters, and the next thing she knew she was in San Francisco, creating curb appeal not for clothing stores but for small restaurants. She was very successful at this, and I wonder if she ever resents the urge that brought her to Agness, Oregon. While Holly enjoys telling me about the mating rituals of the trumpeter swan or the ramifications of the greenhouse effect, she rarely imparts information about herself; most of what I know about her I've had to piece together. If she has fallen short of her goals, if she yearns for something more than me and this house we're constantly mending, she doesn't burden me with it.

~

We are taking Fawn over to Will and Theda's, the owners of Maxine and Crash. Will and Theda built their house out of aluminum cans and plastic jugs and God knows what else. In their backyard is an old washing machine they use as a smoker; in a gutted refrigerator next to it, they raise crayfish. There is always a chicken or two strutting around and several cats, and though I love Will and Theda, I'm getting more and more uneasy at the idea of exposing Fawn to their country chaos.

As usual, Theda is up to her elbows in flour—she bakes pies and cookies for a bakery in town—and Will is out back working on the tractor. For devotees of the simple life, they're the busiest people I know.

"How's our sweet baby girl?" Theda coos, reaching for Fawn with floured hands. Fawn ducks, backs up.

"She's nervous," I apologize. "New surroundings."

"Well, of course she is," Theda says. She settles her hands on her wide hips and beams at Fawn. "She's such a pretty little thing!"

Fawn cranes her neck, taking everything in. Back hunched, tail tight between her legs, she is standing on the linoleum as if she were poised on a flat of eggs.

We have already discussed Fawn's problem with Theda, and she's more than happy to offer her dogs as a course of treatment. "Dogs need dogs," she said, "like people need people." In no time at all, she assured us, Fawn would be running like the wind.

"Are you ready, little one?" she says, grinning, and Fawn looks up at Holly for an answer.

We follow Theda's thick blonde braid and swaying hips out of the house; sure enough, there's a pair of orange chickens pecking up dust near the back steps. "Hold her tight," I whisper to Holly—just in case. The chickens stop feeding; each aim an eye at Fawn, who is trying to slink by without any trouble. Theda stamps her Birkenstock, and they scrabble away. On the other side of the steps, a black cat is lounging in a cracked flowerpot. As we walk past, she stops washing her paw and turns her cool green gaze on Fawn; almost immediately she loses interest and resumes her bath.

"Hey!" Will calls. We look to the left and see him waving from atop the tractor. Will is tall and rail-thin; with his long hair and straggly beard, he reminds me of Jesus. Crash is running circles around the tractor and barking frantically.

"Crash!" Theda yells. The dog stops, turns his head. "Here, Crash!"

Now he is racing toward us, full tilt, flat out. Fawn, seeing what's coming, freezes; Holly crouches down next to her. Theda chuckles and, stepping forward, grabs Crash's collar just before he slams into us.

"Stay," she orders, holding him back; he shivers, whines, tries to squirm forward. "Lie *down*."

This last command has some effect. Tongue lolling, sides heaving, Crash glances up at Theda, then back at Fawn, and, giving up, lowers his belly to the dirt. Fawn, meanwhile, hasn't moved; her ears are flattened to her skull.

"I'll let him go in a minute," Theda says. "He'll be fine." Slowly Holly gets to her feet. With her free hand, Theda ruffles the fur on Crash's neck. "Beast," she declares, and gives us a wink.

When Theda finally lets go of Crash, he shoots over to Fawn and starts sniffing. She doesn't try to flee, she doesn't growl—she just sinks to the ground and stays there, and while his tail swings near her head and his wet nose quivers over her haunches, she looks the other way. She pretends he isn't there.

For the next hour and a half, Fawn doesn't move, not even when Maxine lumbers over and flops down beside her. Next to Fawn, Maxine is more hideous than ever, with that enormous square head and white puckered eye and those gums hanging out of her mouth. Will gives up on the tractor, and the four of us sit on the back steps drinking homemade beer and watching Crash wear himself out: He whimpers at Fawn, he jogs back and forth, he falls on his front legs and barks in her face. But she gives him only an occasional baffled glance, and at last he collapses at our feet.

Theda shrugs. "We'll try again tomorrow."

No one says a word.

~

An hour later, Holly and I are sitting at the kitchen table drinking tea—orange spice for me, burdock for her. She is wearing her big white robe, and her arms emerge from the sleeves like shy, ravaged animals. The eczema has surfaced on her neck and throat now, which is why I doubled her dose of PABA and made the burdock tea extra strong. No one likes the taste of burdock, and I am touched that Holly drinks the bitter brew without complaining. More vitamin E? I am thinking. Brewer's yeast?

It's not like her to sit here idle—she should be reading, or using her carving tools, or drawing up plans for the hall. My stomach tightens as I look at the streaks on her neck, at her arms so thin and red. She is no better, after all these weeks at home. The medicines aren't working, and the dog hasn't helped at all.

As if summoned by my thoughts, Fawn appears in the doorway. There is no escaping those dark, bottomless eyes.

"What does she want?" I mutter, more to myself than to Holly. And I am stunned when Holly answers right away, in a voice flat with truth: "She wants to know what to do with herself. She wants to know how to be a dog."

~

I am not surprised that night to reach out and find Holly gone from our bed. I lie there a moment, picturing her on the porch, her arms encircling her knees, her face turned toward the moon shining behind blue clouds, and then I put on my robe and head down the hall. At the entrance to the kitchen, I stop. The back door is open, and in its frame I see Holly and Fawn sitting on the steps. Holly's arms are clasped around the dog. "You have to run." She is sobbing, her face pressed into Fawn's neck. "Please, please run."

I have seen Holly cry, of course, but not like this.

A slow wedge of fear moves into my chest as I turn and edge back down the hall. There is nothing left to draw on. We are bankrupt, stranded.

~

I leave the house early the next morning, before Holly gets up. I am anxious to get to work, to be in a place where the problems can be solved. Today I need to clean out the compressors and check the bulk food bins—a customer said the oats were stale.

I drive down our dirt road, swerving past the potholes, and turn left into town. Not many kids stop by anymore—we live too far out—but when we had the house on Fulton Street, they were always around. They'd come to view Holly's miniatures, or to learn how to make salt crystals, or to see the rescued wildlife convalescing in our backyard. Children can't get enough of Holly. They drop their guard, say things; they forget she's a grown-up.

Again I imagine her on Fifth Avenue, working behind the plate-glass windows, and I think of the dainty gardens and the mini deserts she fashions now, and I see the way she's pared down her life. From Bergdorf Goodman to the Talking Turtle Day Care Center. From the dictates of businessmen to the needs of children. There must be clues in this, tips I can use to help her, and as I ponder them, I drive right past my store.

I have finished with the compressors and am on my way to the bulk bins when I notice several people standing out front. The store doesn't open for another twenty minutes, but they can't wait. Just being near these herbs and vitamins, just smelling that wheatgrass makes them feel better, fills them with faith and resolve. I unlock the door to my magic kingdom and let them all inside.

People who shop here generally fall into one of two categories: those who exude good health and those who endlessly pursue it. Today there is one bodybuilder who buys a pound of creatine powder and is in and out of the store so fast I feel used; a forty-something woman who buys a half-dozen veggie burgers and looks great in spandex; a teenage boy asking about herbal aphrodisiacs; a pale girl with acne who will wander the aisles for over an hour; and, of course, Rick, the store mascot, a strapping old man who comes in daily for a pint of carrot juice and who I swear has the life span of a redwood.

Today everybody leaves the store happily clutching their antidotes. I have listened and instructed, have drawn straight lines between the complaints and the cures, like those exercises in grammar school where you match up corresponding objects. Not all days are this gratifying, especially lately, and instead of feeling fraudulent, guilty over the prices I'm forced to charge, I am pleased with myself as I lock up Earthly Goods. It *is* a place of magic, of hope, and people like Rick and the spandex woman are walking testimonials to the legitimacy of my trade.

I take my time driving home, reluctant to face Holly and the dog and the mire we're in. Again I picture Holly sobbing on the porch, and I'm appalled by the things I don't know about her. Just how close is she to depletion?

And so I'm amazed to open the front door and find her humming in the hallway. She has a tape measure in her hands and is writing down figures on a piece of paper.

I smile at her. "The diorama?"

She walks up and kisses me. "I'm trying to decide if I should do just one period or a progression of three—Triassic, Jurassic, and Cretaceous."

"The progression," I answer.

"I knew you'd say that," she says.

~

I am slicing up spinach leaves for an omelet, and Holly is sitting at the table looking through her natural history books.

"Hadrosaurs had rookeries like birds," she informs me. "Their nests were ten feet in diameter."

I smack the flat of my knife against a garlic clove and pull off the papery skin. I am learning a lot about dinosaurs. But there is something else I want to talk about right now. I brush the garlic slivers into the hot skillet, and the fragrance fills the kitchen.

"You know," I begin carefully, casually, "maybe it's not important, getting Fawn to run. If she doesn't want to, maybe we shouldn't try. I mean, hasn't she had enough of that?"

"It's not the same thing," Holly says without turning around.

"If we walk her every day," I persist, "and watch her diet, she won't get fat."

Holly has no comment to this, but I see the resolution in her shoulders, and I know I can't change her mind and probably shouldn't try—she's the expert when it comes to injury.

~

We are clearing the dinner dishes from the table when Fawn

enters the kitchen. She doesn't pause on the threshold this time; she walks right in and sits, and then she does something that startles all three of us. She lifts her chin and makes a sound, a single ardent note, something between a howl and a bark, a question and a statement. Afterward, puzzled, she looks behind her, as if she's not sure where the sound came from. A fork slides off the plate in my hands and clatters on the floor. Holly turns to me, her face radiant.

"She's coming around."

~

Fawn's recovery happens by degrees, one tenuous achievement every day or so. Yesterday her tail wagged, not exuberantly and not for long—just a few soft beats against the carpet while Holly was petting her—but a breakthrough nevertheless. And just this morning she walked over to the table where I was doing paperwork and rested her slender muzzle on my thigh. I stared at it the way you would a butterfly that lights, oblivious, on the back of your hand.

Fawn even looks better. Although she hasn't gained weight, she seems more solid, more sure of her place in this house. There is a loosening in her now, as if the tension that bound her, that made her a race dog, is finally letting go.

Ten times a night she ran. Ten times around a floodlit track. Sometimes, when she is sleeping on her bed in the living room, I see her legs twitch, and I wonder if she is still haunted by those nights—or if the dreams are pleasant, if she is running not around a track, muzzled and numbered, but across a vast meadow, achieving in her sleep a freedom otherwise out of reach. People who are paralyzed have dreams like this. Sleep can be a place for solutions.

And Holly is better, too. Maybe it's because of the dog; maybe they struck some bargain that rock-bottom night on the porch. Then again, I can't rule out the PABA, or all that burdock tea. In any event, the rash is leaving. The marvel occurs at night, in time-lapse; each morning is cause to celebrate. It's a drama we've seen many times before, and still we feel triumphant. How long this state of grace will last is a question we don't need answered.

~

Like most long-awaited phenomena, it happens without warning. We are walking along the perimeter of the soccer field, as we do every week—Holly near the fence, me on the inside, and Fawn in perfect step between us. Holly is explaining why dinosaurs could not have been cold-blooded when Fawn stops short. We look down at her, surprised, not yet knowing what it could mean.

She springs forward, checks herself, and with a last glance at Holly she is bounding away, jackknifing over the field. Holly reaches for my arm, and all we can do is watch as Fawn leaves us farther and farther behind. In seconds she has reached the edge of the woods and is turning back, closing in fast, racing without a reason, her body in a full ecstatic stretch high above the ground.

# Survival Skills

I want to come back as a plant. A life above and a life below. No thinking, just finding. Water, food, light.

Maybe not a redwood; that's a long, long life. A sunflower might be fun. One sturdy stalk zooming skyward, pushing fuzzy, heart-shaped leaves, and then the grand finale: a giant yellow flower brimming with seeds. The ending an offering, a promise kept. Half a year on earth and not a single wasted moment.

~

My brother doesn't drive anymore. When he rides with me, I find myself driving more cautiously: hands on the wheel at ten and two, eyes scanning left and right. Every block or so he glances up, then jerks his head back down. His hands, jammed in his lap, rub against each other constantly. He is trying. A few months ago, he couldn't get into a car. Couldn't even say the word.

An accident—that's what most people think. No. Nothing happened—at least nothing we're likely to understand. There he was, driving to work, normal as you and me, when somewhere in his brain a pair of neurons fired, and doubt was born. Had he hit someone?

He checked the mirrors, turned around, circled several times. Nothing in the road, but he couldn't be sure. He may never be sure again.

~

Locomotion. That's our problem. If we stayed in one place, we could grow unerringly, drinking the rain, absorbing the sun, pulling in food with our feet.

With a brain you get options, illusions, second guesses, mistakes. One trifling incident slips into that gray jelly, and, just like that, you're hardwired for trouble. Everything is a matter of association and interpretation; the margin of error is incalculable. The fact that we can't see the forest for the trees doesn't make much sense, considering what we have to work with: The human brain is so disproportionately large that as infants we can't hold our heads up.

The reason we need a brain that big? Language. Our crowning achievement. We are word wizards. Not only can we learn any number of words, we know how to string them together so that we may comfort or seduce, cajole or deride, inspire or coerce, inform or inflame.

Double talk. Slander. Fine print. Filibuster. Language may be getting the better of us.

~

Wendy Mack, my nearest neighbor on this lake, has given up the spoken word. No one around here has heard her speak since the day her daughter died, two years ago this June, of a rampant staph infection. She lost her mind, people said, snapped like a twig.

Aside from Wendy's silence, she seems normal enough to me. Sometimes she brings me cuttings from her garden, sometimes a basket of tomatoes. I just nod and smile and take them from her, figuring that if she's not talking, she's not keen on listening either, at least not to words. Every so often I walk across the tall grass that separates our houses, and we sit in the wicker chairs on her porch and watch the setting sun turn the lake to copper and listen to the crickets and leopard frogs, the occasional jumping trout, the buzz of a dragonfly. Lift away language, and you hear all kinds of things.

Kris, my daughter, has no patience for Wendy. "What is she trying to prove?" she asked me last week. "What's the point? It's like she's trying to punish someone."

"Who knows?" I said. "Maybe she's punishing God by not using the gifts she was given." You'll not believe this, but Wendy used to be a motivational speaker. She lectured all over the country and wrote four books—two of them bestsellers—on how to rouse yourself. I have an autographed copy of her first book, *Yes, You Can!*

Oddly enough, on the opposite shore of this lake, in a yellow house directly across from mine, lives a man who speaks volumes. His name is John Dalrymple, and he used to teach Chaucer and Shakespeare at Northeastern University. I've always been impressed with his prodigious vocabulary, which he still happily exercises, though his sentences are now indecipherable. Several months ago, John fell out of his hayloft and smacked the side of his head on a horse stall. When you ask him how his wife is doing, he is likely to say something along these lines: "Oh, yes, the more the better. One day soon. Biscuits with blackberry jam." I have no idea if he understands the words that flow out of him, but he seems remarkably at peace.

~

Plants communicate with exquisite subtlety. If a tree on the African plain is being ravaged by antelopes, it will send a chemical signal to its neighboring relatives. Instantaneously these other trees will begin manufacturing more tannins, just enough to render them toxic to the herbivores, who, in their own canny way, will seek an alternate food source.

In response to beetle attacks, a conifer will release wads of resin, embalming the marauders. If ground ivy loses its shade, it quickly gets to work toughening and thickening its leaves.

Whatever happens—floods, droughts, bugs, beasts—plants are always making corrections, becoming the best they can be.

~

"Why do you think you hit someone?" I asked my brother.

"I saw a shadow."

"Maybe it was a road sign, or a passing bird."

Eric shook his head firmly. "I felt a bump under the tires."

"Probably just a pothole or a frost heave."

"No. It didn't feel like that. It was more than that."

"But you went back and nothing was there, right?"

He didn't answer, just glared at the floor, his mouth set in a grim line. I had no idea at that point just how often we would have this exchange, or how much time he would start to spend on these frenzied searches. That Eric never saw a body in the road did little to reassure him. Maybe, he reasoned, the victim had crawled away. Maybe another motorist had stopped and picked him up. Maybe an ambulance had already come. Was that a siren in the distance?

Dysperceptions are what they are called: sights and sounds the brain creates to confirm its greatest fears.

~

Field dodder cannot afford doubt. A leafless, thread-like vine, unable to make its own food, it snakes through garden beds, ambushing the innocent. With no energy to spare, dodder must be swift in finding a proximate host in adequate health. The wrong choice, a moment's lag, and the vine perishes.

And yet dodder is next to impossible to kill. "Devil's Hair," gardeners call it. Yank out the thin yellow strands, and the smallest remnants persist. And forget about saving the strangled host—a prize dahlia, say; the poor thing is already gone.

~

In college I had a roommate who was afraid of wind. Breezy days would turn her wide-eyed and quiet. On gusty days she took Valium and stayed indoors. Gale-force winds would chase her under the covers, where she hugged her knees and moaned and cried. Naturally, I couldn't use the fan I had brought from home and had to keep it out of sight.

There is a word for the fear of wind. Ancraophobia. In fact, there is a name for nearly any phobia you can think of: the fear of otters, garlic, knees. There is a fear of beautiful women. There is even a fear of sunshine.

What a comfort for the afflicted, to see their illnesses respected with names. I'm glad that someone is keeping up the list.

~

Orchids! Over 25,000 species in the wild, each one fabulous simply because it manages to exist.

The quickest route to extinction is cross-pollination; to avoid this threat, each orchid variety seduces a particular insect, bird, or butterfly, offering up whatever scents or shapes or colors the creature craves. An orchid pollinated by a hummingbird is likely to have red tubular flowers filled with nectar, while an orchid fertilized by carrion beetles comes in shades of brown and smells like rotting meat.

Imagine being that sure of yourself: Sweet or stinking, you claim the right to be here.

~

We spook too easily—a throwback to the time we were prey. Nowadays this hair-trigger alarm is more trouble than benefit, but there it is anyway, lodged deep within the brain, steeped in ancestral memories.

The truth is, our noggins are still evolving. We can't help it that we see a stick and think *snake!* Three thousand years ago, the brain's hemispheres were not even integrated: One side "spoke," and the other side "listened." Which goes a long way toward explaining all those oracles and talking gods.

My brother began calling hospitals to ask if any accident victims had been admitted. When he started phoning the highway patrol several times a day, he wound up in a rehab center outside of Boston, where he stayed for three months in a sage-green room, eating nutritious meals and learning ways to calm himself. Because his fears began behind the wheel, that's where they launched his lessons. "Car," he wrote, over and over, filling the pages of a legal pad; then he had to say the word; then he had to look at pictures of cars; then he had to carry the pictures in his pocket; and so on. Believe me, it's been a long journey to the passenger seat; I couldn't be more proud of him.

~

Bull's Horn Acacia is a tree in South America that sports giant, hollow, curving thorns. Attracted to these formidable thorns are stinging ants that drill their way inside and take up residence. If a branch is disturbed—typically by destructive leaf-cutter ants—the stinging ants will race out of the thorns and sting the attackers to death. In return for this service, the tree provides its defenders with shelter, nectar, and, as if not forgetting anything, tiny protoplasm-rich nodules that ensure complete nutrition.

If we ever saw the big picture—if our minds could accommodate, even for a split second, the terrible balance of life on this planet—we would surely be frightened out of our wits.

No way are we ready for custodianship.

~

So, plants. No brain, no fear. Just the urge to grow. The right to be here. I'd love to come back as a lilac, but a stinking orchid would be okay, too.

# A Sea Change

My mother lights another Winston and, eying me closely, blows the smoke out the side of her mouth. She is circling, looking for a way into my confidence.

"So she's moving out?"

"Tomorrow." I am watching the frantic maneuvers of a hummingbird confused by the red plastic flowers.

She tilts her head; I can feel her frowning. "Did something happen, Jenny? Did you have a fight?"

I shake my head no.

She leans forward, lowers her voice. "Another woman?"

I look at the black windows of her sunglasses. Cosmetic surgery has pulled out most of her wrinkles, and her face, shiny and taut, is straining with anticipation. Her glossy red lips are parted. Even her hair is shimmering, waiting.

I know she blames me for losing Antonia. I don't fix myself up, she contends, don't pay enough attention to my clothes and my nails.

She cannot imagine how hard I tried—first my methods and then some of hers. How can I explain that it wasn't my fault, that I was up against an octopus and never stood a chance?

It started, of course, at the aquarium. Everything was fine until Antonia got a job at the Monterey Bay Aquarium. Not two weeks later I brought some oysters home, and when I put them on the table she blanched, nearly knocked the chair over getting to her feet. That was the beginning of the end.

Which is pretty ironic considering how we met. Imagine a lovely, dark-haired woman sitting alone in a restaurant. She is watching the sun melt into the Pacific. Her wineglass blazes in the orange light as she raises it to her lips. On the table is a plate of oysters, her second.

It was only by chance that I saw her. I came out of the kitchen for a club soda, and there she was, stunning as a coral reef.

From behind a vase of forsythia I watched her lift each shivering oyster from its icy bed, and even then I could feel the undertow, could see the water rising. There was nothing I could do but flip my apron to the clean side and head straight for her table.

Striking up a conversation was easy enough. There were the oysters, all twelve of which I had pried open, not to mention the mixed greens I had tossed for her, the focaccia I had made. Everything she put in her mouth had first been in my hands.

And so I asked how she liked the oysters and told her they were Quilcenes, fresh from Tomales Bay, and then I mentioned the Olympias I was getting in and asked if she'd ever tried them. She had the most provocative lips I'd ever seen. She smiled a lot and nodded here and there, and if she thought my presence in the dining room was odd (and it was), she didn't let on; maybe she was flirting, too. In any case, she came back for my bivalves every Friday afternoon. The waiters, who caught on quickly, would let me know the minute she arrived, and each time I saw her, backlit in that window, my stomach would start to do flip-flops. Sometimes I had trouble with her oysters because my hands would be shaking so much. I must have opened over a hundred of them before I finally got the nerve to ask her out.

Things fell into place, as they generally do in the beginning. Antonia was thirty-one, and I was just a couple years older. We were both a bit love-weary, having been down that road more than once, and while we didn't exactly hold back, we didn't rush headlong either. It took us four months to get those three little words out of the way, and another two months went by before she moved in with me. This last step was probably the easiest, as she was living in a thin-walled, overpriced apartment in Salinas and I had a house near the beach to offer, one of those whimsical cottages with a sloping rooftop and small, arched doorways. From the street it looks fine, but if you come up the walk you can see the moss in the cedar shingles and the mildew under the eaves, and if you aren't careful you can twist your ankle on the long yellow slugs that slide through the calla lilies. There isn't one thing my mother likes about this house, and I think she hates the lilies most of all. Funeral flowers, she calls them. Big leaky funnels. Bees fly in, she says, and never come out.

Antonia, on the other hand, loved this place. On her first visit here, she sank into the frayed green sofa and looked at the clutter of books and driftwood and said it felt like camp. Time after time I would find her running her hand over the smooth dents in the mahogany table or opening the linen closet just to smell the sheets and towels. From my bedroom window the ocean is a blue rectangle a half mile away, but the briny scent lives in every crack and corner of the house. I was brought up on this air and would probably languish without it.

Antonia was a craftswoman when I met her. She'd gather up sea debris—lustrous bits of abalone, gleaming shark's teeth—and fashion them into jewelry that she sold to the tourist shops. I cleared out the small bedroom my mother once used for sewing, and that's where Antonia set up shop. I liked the fact that she worked at home;

I suppose it bolstered my sense of security. The truth is, I never had much influence over Antonia, and I knew it.

She was beautiful, for one thing—heart-stopping, jaw-dropping, told-you-so beautiful—and that alone should have kept me at bay. Even her name caused me worry—who can possess a woman called Antonia? And then there was her silence, her way of leaving a question unanswered, a quirk that began to unhinge me.

I might have shown better judgment, might have been able to save myself if it hadn't been for our sex life. I have known bedroom Olympians, women who could write manuals on the subject. Antonia wasn't one of them. Indifferent to performance, she would lose herself on a single spot. Her hand would stroke some part of me, over and over, until the world fell away and I was held aloft and breathless. Or, locking her gaze on mine, she would move against me, so slowly, so deliberately, that my body would tremble in preparation. Whatever she did carried me away, always to the same astonishing region. Sex with Antonia was a place.

And our meals—oh, how we feasted! Blinis for breakfast. Mussels at midnight. Artichokes in bed at high noon. Antonia was an avid eater. About the only thing she shunned was meat, which was fine with me: I'd seen enough bloody aprons in my time and was ready to give up mammals myself.

So there we were, loving and feasting, happy as clams, until the day Antonia came out of her shop and said she'd like to do some volunteer work at the Monterey Bay Aquarium. They needed people to help monitor the crowds and make sure the children didn't leap into the bat ray pool or grab something they weren't supposed to. I thought it was a great idea. After tinkering with broken shells and body parts, she could spend some time with living creatures.

Antonia was probably the most dedicated volunteer the aquarium ever had. In her zeal to learn she must have logged fifty hours a week, moving beyond the touch tanks and gaining access to the research labs. At first I was happy for her, delighted to see her so enthralled, but I began to miss our time together—and then came the trouble with food.

It wasn't just oysters; she gave up all sea life, everything that clung, scuttled, drifted, or swam. Which didn't mean I had to, of course, but after sharing shellfish in the moonlight, eating them by myself seemed somehow pathetic. And naturally I didn't want to offend, didn't want the smell of steaming mollusks wafting through the house. It was much simpler to brush up on my vegetarian cooking and eat my seafood at the restaurant.

With all that diligence at the aquarium and, let's face it, the passport of her looks, Antonia got on the payroll in no time. They even enrolled her in a scuba diving class so that she could help feed and care for the fish, a position not typically available to business majors. When coaxed, she would offer up snippets of her workday: the baby otter that refused to swim on its back, the jellyfish that glowed in the dark like small, floating airports. But what she found most beguiling, what she mentioned most often, were the octopuses. The way they watched you, she explained, with those big yellow eyes moving on stalks. You could see, in the black rectangle of their pupils, a spark of intelligence, a hint of something canny and unfathomable. If they trusted you, she said, they would pull themselves out of the bottles they lived in and, extending a tentative arm, they would start to touch you, all over, their suckers tasting and smelling at once. My first thought was, *How horrible*, and then I became alarmed: I didn't want anyone tasting and smelling Antonia. They liked to be stroked in return, she went on, and they were especially fond of eating out of her hand. "What do you feed them?" I asked. She shrugged. "Lobsters, crab, shrimp." All my favorites.

Mornings used to be the best part of the day. Cappuccinos and

Bach and plenty of time before I had to be at the restaurant. We woke up leisurely, making love while the fog-soaked pines dripped outside the window. Now there was barely time for coffee before Antonia was up and out the door. Mute with longing, I would watch her get dressed: those long legs, the supple back, the soft brown sweep of her hair.

She wasn't interested in making jewelry anymore and had packed up all her silver and solder and baby sand dollars. Now the shelves of that room were lined with books, dozens of them, all about the sea. After she left each morning I would go into her marine library, select a volume, and take it back to bed with me. I wanted to learn the habits of my rivals.

I could see why she admired the octopuses so: There isn't much they can't do. If an arm is lost, they can grow another; in less than a second, they can change their color; they can pull twenty times their own weight; and they can ooze through openings no bigger than their eyeballs.

For a while I thought my humanness would hold her, that an octopus, however spectacular, could not usurp me. But then I started thinking about Jane Goodall, enraptured for a quarter century by a gang of chimpanzees, and I realized I might be in trouble.

Most of my friends worked in the mornings, and without Antonia I found myself adrift. About once a week I began to visit my mother. After my father's death several years ago, she'd signed the house over to me and moved to a sunny condo in the valley, well beyond the reach of rust and slugs. Thanks to insurance policies and inheritances, she didn't have to work, and invariably I would find her reading the paper on her deck, happily surrounded by her vinyl geraniums.

I always wondered why I came. It wasn't as if she offered any comfort, although I know she tried, in her fashion. "Antonia's a very feminine girl," she would say, and then, by way of help: "Why don't you grow out your hair—it's been short for years." Or, "Why don't you wear a skirt once in a while—you have nice legs." It was no use trying to explain that the rules she applied to her own life might not be relevant to mine. "Love is love," she'd say, and for that I suppose she deserves some credit.

~

The octopuses at the aquarium live in mayonnaise jars and clay pots. For some reason they like to decorate the area around their homes, and so the divers supply them with shells and bricks, cheap jewelry and old boots—they are not fussy about the nature of the paraphernalia.

You can't fool an octopus. It can sense the mood of a diver by her chemical emanations, and if the diver is nervous or aggressive, the creature will not budge from its nook. Antonia could always entice them. As soon as she appeared, they shot out of their niches and floated over to her. She was so good at calming the new arrivals that the aquarium put her in charge of them, made her the octopus ambassador.

I noticed that Antonia had lost some weight. This no-kill diet wasn't giving her enough calories, and when I cautioned her about it, she looked right through me, her mind on other things. She kept drifting away from my questions and comments, not out of rudeness, I think, but because she was losing the need for speech, forgetting she was on dry land.

I tried to fatten her up with roasted vegetable pastas and wild mushroom risotto, but cooking for her wasn't much fun anymore. One day I made a nice tarragon mayonnaise and steamed up a couple of those colossal Castroville artichokes. Antonia's face turned mournful when I set them on the table.

"What's wrong?" I said, trying to keep the impatience out of my voice.

"Did you know," she murmured, "that if you let these things grow, they turn into huge purple flowers?"

I slapped down my oven mitt. "People have to eat, Tonia. Something has to die."

She did eventually start eating the damn thing, but it brought her no pleasure, and as I regarded her from across the table, all I could think about was the way we used to lie in bed, naked and insatiable, and strip those meaty globes petal by petal.

Antonia never came to the restaurant anymore, and I don't know why it took me so long to see the implications of this, to understand that she didn't want to share in the carnage that was my career. I should have seen right away that a woman devoted to protecting fish cannot live with a woman who filets them.

Harder still, she was turning away in bed. "Sweet dreams," she'd murmur, patting my shoulder and offering me her back. Marooned in the dark, I would moor myself to her, find solace in the perfume of her hair.

~

The aquarium was a place I rarely visited—too many hard feelings stood between me and the entrance. And then there were the swarms of children to contend with, the constant campaign of noise. But I was ready to brave all that. I needed to observe Antonia with her eight-armed admirers, to witness what went on in those underwater chambers.

Like everyone else, I lingered in front of the kelp forest, eerily beautiful in the morning light, and as I watched the leathery brown ribbons swaying in the currents, the chains of bubbles and the silver fish, I could imagine the relief a diver must feel: a single plunge, and all history is banished, blame lifted, anguish ended.

I pressed on, unnerved by the coupling of elements, the terrible subjection of Plexiglas. Seven inches from my face, a grouper the size of a sofa appeared, and then an ocean sunfish, stately as an airship. On another wall, a regiment of barracuda streamed past, followed by a shark, restless and desolate. There was so much sea life vying for attention that I had to look at the floor, rest my eyes on something that wasn't alive.

The octopus exhibit was drawing the biggest crowds, and I had no trouble finding it. I am five foot eight and not frail, quite an advantage in a roomful of spectators. There were children packed in front, breathing and whispering. I could smell the baby shampoo and the candy on their breath, and the colognes and hair sprays of the adults behind me. I didn't like being jammed in with these people, so close to their pores and whiskers and cigarette smoke. But all that faded when I saw Antonia, just a few feet away, immune in her world of water.

Slim and lithesome in her black-and-yellow wetsuit, she looked more fish than human. Evidently she had just served up dinner. Three octopuses were busy eating, delicately plucking their lobster shells clean. A fourth octopus, apparently more interested in Antonia than a meal, had anchored itself to her. An audiotape was playing, informing us as we watched: "An octopus will take up to four hours to eat a lobster, leaving the shell perfectly intact." Great, I thought: another talent. The octopus attached to Antonia was running the tip of an arm across her face and neck. And she, in some weird communion, was likewise stroking the creature's lolling head. "Each arm is covered with more than two hundred extremely sensitive sucker discs, and each disc may have ten thousand neurons to handle both taste and touch." What sort of stimulation was that animal getting?

The octopus with Antonia was the largest of the group, about four feet across, with a mottled brown hide and white spots down each arm. I couldn't take my eyes off its hideous head, just skin around a brain. " ... the most complex of all the invertebrates, capable of gauging its surroundings and transforming its body shape, pattern, color, and texture in a fraction of a second."

I watched for as long as I could. Antonia never once acknowledged the crowd; she was too engrossed in her aquatic Romeo. I don't know how a biologist would classify their behavior, but it was clear to me that she was making love to that beast, touching it in a way she hadn't touched me in a very long time.

Driving home, I started thinking about the others. Did Jane Goodall break someone's heart when she loaded up her rucksack and flew to Africa? I knew now that it could happen, that a woman could find some higher truth in the wet brown eyes of a chimp. I could see them, side by side in a tree, quietly sharing a sunset. Dian Fossey was seduced by gorillas, Joy Adamson by a pride of lions. And men, too, were swept away, stunned by the might of grizzly bears, bewitched by the cry of wolves.

There was no retrieving Antonia; I was way out of my depth. Lying against her back that night, I took a deep breath and asked her when she was leaving. She shrank a little in my arms, and I passed through millennia, through bottomless black oceans, until she finally answered: "Soon."

~

Packing took no time at all: some clothes, some books, her scuba gear. Antonia had done nothing, I realized, to suggest any permanence here—never pruned or planted, never hung a picture or bought a dish towel. She was simply fastened to this place, like a starfish to a pier, and now that her evolution is complete, she is casting off. Leaving this house is hard for her, probably harder than leaving me. What a pleasing harbor it must have been: the soggy shingles, the slippery lilies, the braided rugs embedded with sand, the smell of old canvas in the cupboards and closets.

She is moving to Seattle, where the octopuses grow to fifteen feet. So pure is her love for these animals, how can I hold a grudge? To console myself I think about food, about all the dishes I'm going to make again, in my own kitchen. Sushi. Thai squid. Glazed salmon. Sometimes I even conjure up meat: the thinnest slice of prosciutto wrapped around a wedge of peach.

~

Warm, sweet air from the laundry vent blows up to the deck. The hummingbird, frustrated, has made a beeline for the horizon. My mother is waiting for an answer.

"No," I tell her, "it wasn't another woman. It was"—I flounder a moment—"her work."

My mother's mouth tightens slightly, and I notice the tiny vertical lines crowding her upper lip, no doubt the next target for her plastic surgeon. She is not buying this. Either she doesn't believe I am being honest with her, or she thinks I've been duped and is sorry for me.

"You know," she begins, "I never much cared for that girl. So quiet, and that food thing."

I shake my head. "Mom, no."

We are quiet then, having reached yet another dead end. I look at the pearly pink lacquer on her toenails and the expensive leather sandals she is wearing and contrast them with my own neglected toes, my worn-out, dime-store thongs, and it seems to me that we are like most mothers and daughters: not quite what the other had in mind. Still, of all the places I could be this morning, I am here.

"Well, kiddo," my mother says, falling back on the safety of her favorite adage, "there are plenty of other fish in the sea."

I smile at this, which she misinterprets as a wave of optimism, and encouragingly she beams back at me.

# What Gretel Knows

Gretel is a six-year-old beagle and the keeper of my secrets. All but one of these secrets she uncovered easily, in friendly doggy fashion, using her superb senses. Sam, for instance: She smelled him on my hands and face, even after I'd washed up. Or maybe it was my step that tipped her off; maybe she heard the guilt in my gait. Or was it the shame on my face, plain as day to a dog as wise as Gretel?

A dog's mind is too wide and pure for judgment. Gretel's foremost concern is my happiness, which she endlessly encourages me to pursue. Still, there are times when I walk in the house after being with Sam, and she gives me a long, questioning look. Do you know what you're doing? she telegraphs. Are you sure this won't wreck our lives?

More than once she has found me in the kitchen helping myself to a juice glass of chardonnay at two or three o'clock in the morning. There I am, sitting at the table in my robe, backlit by the stove light, then click, click, click, I hear her nails on the linoleum and she is standing in front of me, her brown eyes kind and searching.

Last month she caught me reading Hannah's diary. I wasn't

looking for punishable offenses; I was only hunting for clues as to why my daughter despises me. By the time Gretel walked into the room and saw the green binder in my hands, I had read nearly half the entries.

These secrets must weigh on Gretel, which might be the reason she sighs as she does. All dogs sigh, but Gretel's long groans seem to come from the depths of her being, as if she is trying to get free of herself, to utter the unutterable.

~

Even as a young woman I was not especially keen on sex. In this respect, at least, Alan and I are a lucky match. No more than twice a month we make good-natured, uncomplicated love, a ration that suits me just fine and seems to keep Alan running like a top. Given this agreeable arrangement, I can't explain what happened between Sam and me, or why it's still happening. I love Alan. I do.

Sam is a lepidopterist. While he lectures on both butterflies and moths, he is especially devoted to moths and has written three books about them, including a children's guide. In search of exotic species, he travels all over the world; last winter, in Singapore, he came across a dozen or so giant Atlas moths. He said you could hear the whoosh of their wings as they cruised the cherry trees.

We met on a muggy, moonless night in August. Sam had run an ad in the local paper inviting anyone interested to join him in Turner's Park for a moth hunt. I knew next to nothing about moths and had no idea what this excursion would entail, but it sounded more interesting than the book I was reading, certainly better than anything on television. It was indeed a night of surprises, the first one being the number of people who showed up—sixteen in all, half of them young boys, the other half adult women, my age or older.

Sam's preparations amazed me. Earlier that day, he had painted a syrupy patch on three dozen trees along the trail, then marked each tree with an orange ribbon. Moth bait, he called it, a homemade elixir that contained stale beer, brown sugar, and rotten watermelons. Guided by our flashlights, we walked quietly along the path, stopping to inspect each painted tree. Sam had covered the lens of his flashlight with red cellophane—less disturbing than white light, he said—and it was true that the moths didn't stir when he aimed the beam on the trees. Some of the trees had nothing on them but slugs and carpenter ants, but many hosted some kind of moth, the names of which Sam whispered into the night: "Glossy Black Idia … Copper Underwing … Cloaked Marvel." Captivated, we studied the creatures with budding reverence, as if in those deep woods we had all fallen under a spell. Why had I never noticed how exquisite they were, how intricate their markings? Why had I never seen, before this night, their furry little faces?

"That's an Oldwife Underwing," murmured Sam, shining his light on a charcoal-colored moth that had opened its wings, revealing another set below, twin brown fans with bright orange stripes. Hidden jewelry.

"Do you think we'll see any Luna moths?" I asked as we walked to the next tree.

"Too late for Lunas," Sam said. He has a deep voice, almost mournful; his walk is slow and long-strided. He is, in fact, exactly what you might think of when you think *lepidopterist*—lean, bespectacled, with a long, narrow nose and deep lines running down his cheeks. "And they wouldn't be on these trees anyway," he added. "They don't eat."

"They don't *eat!*" blurted one of the boys.

"They can't," Sam replied. "They don't have mouths." His words hung in the darkness, allowing us to absorb them.

I couldn't imagine the things he knew. At home in the dark, here was a man who was spending his time on earth learning the names and habits of moths, a man for whom these fluttery, powdery bugs were reason enough to be alive. Though months would pass before we mated, I was drawn to him that very first night.

~

Eva is coming for a visit. I haven't seen her in more than two years, other than in some family photos she e-mails now and then. At thirty-seven, she is more stunning than ever. Her hair is a dazzling silver-blonde, and her face, slimmer now, has acquired new chic. Most amazing is her smile. She always had a pretty smile, but at some point in the last decade it turned radiant. While I am being subtracted, the years are heaping riches on Eva.

Growing up, you couldn't tell we were sisters. Eva was a giggly, curly-haired towhead. She loved her dolls and party dresses; I favored books and sturdy boots. As the younger sibling, her devotion for me was simple and unquestioning: Wherever I went, she tried to follow. I can see her still, tagging behind me, wearing some silly dress and those white patent leather shoes, which of course were useless in the woods. I would sit on a fallen tree and pull out my notepad, and a moment later she'd be there, too, a few feet away, keeping a careful distance so I wouldn't shoo her home. I came to the woods to write poems, or try to, and Eva knew she had to be quiet. Soon enough, though, she'd start to hum or sing, or she'd knock her heels against the log and start asking questions, and that would be that.

What I like most to recall are the nights we shared, warm summer nights, sweet with jasmine, thick with stars. We ran through our neighborhood like savages, making a game of the darkness, using it to hide in, to banish the rules of daytime. Eva wanted to know everything: what made fireflies glow, why the moon kept changing. "It goes around the earth," I explained, "over and over, so we only see parts of it. The light on the moon is the sun's reflection." She could not have understood all the things I told her, but she hung on my words and believed what I said. Who has ever loved me with more conviction?

Eva has two boys and is married to a commercial realtor who makes gobs of money. They've been together for a while now, and so far so good, but I'm wary. Frank is handsome, alarmingly so. Men that good-looking have power beyond measure—who knows what they're capable of? On their wedding day I gave him a hug, then looked into his glacier-blue eyes and said, "Take care of my sister." I wasn't smiling. There was some dried frosting on his cheek, spots of champagne on his tie. He regarded me blearily, then broke into a gorgeous grin. "You bet I will," he nearly shouted.

We'll see.

~

There is no mention of me in Hannah's diary. Evidently I am not worth comment. I know that teenage girls are a moody lot, that I shouldn't make too much of this, but I can't help envy Eva her boys, who seem, in their straightforward way, so much kinder. I have no doubt that they will take care of Eva in her dotage. God forbid I should ever be at the mercy of Hannah.

When I was pregnant with Hannah I used to imagine the two of us strolling hand-in-hand through meadows and forests; I saw us sharing sunsets, gazing at the Big Dipper. Even before she was out of her crib I knew this wasn't likely. Hannah wanted action: talking toys, musical mobiles. Her favorite possession was a pink plastic phone on which she babbled for hours and dragged everywhere. Now she has a shiny red cell phone to which she is similarly attached.

Not long ago I was sitting at the kitchen table looking through a book I had borrowed from Sam. In front of me was a photograph of a Verdant Hawk moth, a species from Africa. I was admiring its powerful green wings and sturdy body when Hannah's sudden voice startled me.

"You and your moths!" she said with a shudder. "Why don't you study butterflies? They're a lot prettier, and you wouldn't have to be outside in the middle of the night."

"Actually," I said, "there are lots of pretty moths." I looked up from the book. Hannah was standing beside me, her dark hair hanging in her eyes. "And quite a few of them fly in the daytime."

"Whatever," she murmured, walking out of the room.

Maybe we're like moths and butterflies, Hannah and I, sharing a few traits but living in separate domains. It helps to think so, at any rate. To believe this divide is not our fault.

~

By day I manage a gift shop, a faux log cabin heavily scented with potpourri and filled with the sort of things tourists expect to find in a small New Hampshire town: maple syrup, hardwood bowls, pine-scented pillows, miniature birch bark canoes. Selling these quaint curios doesn't require much effort, and in the slower months I have ample time to write—not that I do much of that anymore. After college I did manage to publish a handful of poems in some decent journals, but at some point I lost momentum; then I lost heart.

Alan is a sales rep for a large organic fertilizer company. Nine months of the year he travels the byways of New England, stopping at nurseries and box stores. He doesn't grouse about his job, but I know the driving must get tiresome, if not hazardous—and how many times a day must he repeat himself, explaining the benefits of microorganisms and carbon-based compounds?

I've wondered if Alan, in his travels, ever has any dalliances—surely there's plenty of opportunity. It's not hard to picture that blue Sebring nosing in and out of seaside motels, trysts as trackless as windblown leaves. I have seen other women, friends even, look at him with a certain avidity. He still has a boyish smile and all his hair, and for someone who spends so much time behind a steering wheel, Alan is remarkably fit, thanks to those gadgets he takes with him: chin-up bars that fit in door frames, stretchy bands that hook around his feet.

Sam and I were in his backyard that first time, studying the moths that came to a sheet he had strung between two trees. In front of this sheet hung a bug zapper he had disabled—the black light inside was all he wanted. (Sam loathes bug zappers and refers to them as "indiscriminate killers.")

What we were hoping to see on that cool May night was a Luna moth, though Sam said the chances were slim as the species was in danger.

"Why?" I asked. "Pesticides?"

He nodded. "The Bt they've put in corn seed—the pollen goes everywhere."

We sat in lawn chairs under the stars, blankets on our laps; Sam's white sneakers shone in the grass. We could hear small frogs leaping into the pond at the edge of Sam's property. The treetops were black against the sky, and the night smelled of pine and marsh.

We'd been sitting there for nearly an hour, watching the various moths and bats that flew through the night, when what we wanted to see came floating across the yard. The soft green glow of its wings was unmistakable; you could almost believe it had come by way of the moon. I caught my breath as it sailed over our heads, trailing those long tips, before deftly landing on the sheet. We both rose at the same instant and approached the creature slowly. "A female," Sam said. "The males have thicker antennae."

"It's amazing," I whispered. I peered at the luminous wings, edged in maroon, and the four transparent spots that resembled large eyes, a device to fool predators.

"I wonder if she'll attract any males," I said. I had read about moth pheromones and knew that the scent from a single female could draw males from several miles away.

"She's already mated," Sam said. "The females mate even before they make their first flight, then they find a tree and lay their eggs. This one has done all that."

"And she doesn't eat, right? How much time does she have left?"

Sam shrugged. "Not much. Maybe a day or two. Their life span is about a week."

I smiled at him. "What a tidy life. You're born, you mate, you fly, you lay eggs, and then you're just a lovely thing. Free to be. And you don't even know you're going to die."

That was the moment Sam turned to me and touched my arm. His fingers rested there, lightly. In the glow of the black light, his face was serious, questioning, and it didn't take long for me to close the space between us. That's where we made love that first night, on a blanket in the wet grass, not four feet away from a Luna moth. I had no second thoughts; I had no thoughts at all. It was as if we, too, were running out of time and only doing what we must.

Two years later, I don't know why we persist. Falling upon each other on a pheromone-drenched night in May is one thing, but where is the urgency in our random couplings now?

"What are you thinking about?" Sam asked last week. We were in bed, and he was idly running his hand down my side. I had my back to him. His dresser was a couple feet away, a gray sock sticking out of the top drawer.

"It's different now," I told him.

"What's different?"

"Us." His hand paused on my hipbone. I stared at the dresser. "It feels like stealing for no reason."

Sometimes I think that what I like most about the affair is being in Sam's cottage, which is musty and dark and nothing like the house I live in. There are books and papers everywhere, odd pieces of furniture covered in snug coats of dust. Sam lives like the bachelor he is (he was married, briefly, in his twenties), with a clutter of dishes in the sink and sheets that need laundering. This peaceful disarray soothes me—I've never so much as washed a cup, nor does Sam expect me to. Sam makes no demands. He is happy to see me when I can manage it; beyond that, I don't kid myself. If Sam had the chance to see a Black Witch moth or me, I know I'd be curling up with a book.

~

Gretel never gives up on me. Every day of her life, she waits for me to have some fun. She cannot understand why something so easy should be so elusive.

"Like this," she seems to say, dropping onto her forelegs, rump in the air, tail wagging. "Just do this!"

Obliging her, I will sometimes start to run; I'll put some excitement in my voice, and she will leap and bark encouragingly. It doesn't matter to her if this eagerness isn't genuine. She only wants the effort.

"Does your hip ever bother you?" I once asked Eva. "I mean, does it hurt?"

She shrugged. "Only if it gets really cold, and it doesn't get that cold in Mill Valley."

I nodded, looked away. "Do you remember that day?" I said, my heart pounding. "Do you remember how it happened?"

Eva frowned in concentration. "Not really. I was running, right? And then I fell? I *do* remember the ambulance, and I remember the nurses at the hospital and how nice they were."

Eva doesn't talk about her limp (she says she scarcely thinks of it), though there must have been plenty of times, growing up, when she was embarrassed by it, or hindered—two of her best friends were cheerleaders, and that was just the sort of activity my gregarious sister might have signed up for.

When I was a teenager I used to make lists of things that Eva would never become: dancer, gymnast, tennis pro. It would not be tragic, I reasoned, if these activities were out of her reach; there were so many other avenues she could explore—no end, really, to what she could do.

One day, adding to the list of could-nots, I wrote down "marathon runner," which got me thinking about running in general and what sort of events, over the course of a lifetime, people might need to run from. Mad dogs. Muggers. Fire. How many other things?

Eva couldn't run for her life. That was the one I couldn't write down.

~

We have no idea how it happens, how the death of a caterpillar gives life to a moth. Here is this plump green crawler, busily sawing through sassafras leaves, shedding one loose-fitting suit after another, until, with a hidden nudge from nature, it stops chewing and gets down to the business of dying. If the weather is still warm, it will spin a silk sheath and wrap itself in a leaf; if winter is approaching, it secretes a hard shell and spends the cold months underground. In either case, the bug begins to disintegrate, bit by bit, leg by leg, breaking apart in its own digestive juices. But then, in this wretched dead sea, some rebel cells start swimming. Having served no purpose in the larval life, they are finally called to muster. Their task: to make something marvelous, a creature—*with wings!*

I can't walk past a moth anymore without stopping to peer at it, to marvel over its tiny, unfathomable dramas. Some nights I walk out on my porch just to see who's showed up at the light. Sam says that moths are not attracted to light so much as they are pulled into it; stunned, they stay there. Turn off the light, and they break away.

I do that. There are times when I step off my lighted porch and slip into the welcoming shadows alongside the house. The night absorbs me. There, under impartial stars, in a perfect wedge of darkness, I disappear.

~

Last night Gretel found me in the kitchen again. At that late hour she doesn't hold much hope for play, and so she approached me quietly, casting an eye on my juice glass of wine before sitting down next to my chair. "Who's a pretty girl?" I said. She lifted the velvet flaps of her ears and fixed me in her amber gaze. We sat like this, adoring each other, until she let out a small sigh and lowered her belly to the floor, setting her chin on my foot.

I don't know how long I sat there, my gaze on the sweet dome of Gretel's head, before I pushed back my chair and stood up.

"Know what I want?"

Gretel got to her feet and looked up at me.

"I want a real wineglass." I crossed the kitchen, plucked one from the cupboard, and poured the rest of my wine into it.

"And how about some light?" I said, snapping on the overhead. The room sprang into being. Suddenly there were things I might do.

I pulled a notepad and pen from the drawer under the phone and brought them to the table. "Let's plan some menus, okay?" Gretel wagged her tail. I dropped my voice to a whisper. "Or maybe, *maybe*, we'll write a poem." She settled back down near my chair but kept her eyes on me.

"And stop worrying about me and Sam," I said. "We're on our way out."

~

One day, years ago, when Alan was gone and Hannah was away at summer camp, I drank the better part of a bottle of wine before slipping off the sofa and onto the rug next to Gretel. She was barely more than a puppy then and probably not ready to hear this story.

"Eva was wearing those stupid shoes," I began. "I don't know how many times I told her not to wear her patent leather shoes in the woods. I *warned* her."

Gretel yawned nervously.

"She wanted to look at my books, and I told her she couldn't. She was six! I knew she'd wind up drawing in them, coloring in them." I paused, and Gretel, seeing an out, tried to slink away; I caught her jowls in my hands and made her look at me.

"She started to cry—that's when our mother came in. She told me to stop being so selfish, and then she slapped me! That's when I ran out of the room."

"I was hurt," I went on, trying to make Gretel understand. "She'd never slapped me before. I ran all the way to the woods, and that's when I heard Eva calling me. She was following me, running as fast as she could. She was wearing her yellow dress and those stupid shoes, and she was holding onto this ragdoll she had." I trailed off, lost in that morning, and Gretel gave a whimper.

"I wouldn't stop," I said, tightening my hold on Gretel, "and she wouldn't stop. Every time I looked back, she was still coming after me, her face all red, that doll jerking in her hand. I cut over, started running along the creek bank."

Gretel squirmed and rolled her eyes away from me.

"I thought she'd give up—it was slippery—but she kept coming. I could hear her crying and calling my name. I finally stopped, only it was too late. She was falling." My eyes filled with tears then. "I could see her yellow dress, rolling over and over. A tree shattered her hip."

Gretel swung her gaze back to my face, and I let go of her.

"They thought it would heal okay, but it didn't."

For a moment neither one of us moved, and then Gretel collapsed on the rug and gave a long, deep sigh. What else could she do?

# The Spider in the Sink

Ants are easy. Their very numbers make them expendable. They goad you into it, the way they march across the kitchen and besiege your sugar bowl in broad daylight. Who wouldn't pick up a sponge and decimate them?

But what about the spider in the sink? No bigger than an aspirin, it shrinks in terror when your hand approaches. Somewhere the little fellow made a wrong turn; it does not want to be in your sink, and now it can't get out. With a splash of water, you could send it down the dark hell of your plumbing; you wouldn't even have to look. There is a chance the wee bug would never cross your mind again.

You don't take that chance. You tear off a piece of toilet paper and nudge it beneath the creature, and in your nightgown you walk through the house and out the back door, and you shake the tissue over a bush. One day perhaps this spider will eat the aphids off your rosebuds. But that is not why you save it.

~

Your husband did not wave before he pulled out of the driveway, and your thoughts keep snagging on this. Every morning you wait for that gesture, his hand arcing out the window, and today he simply drove off. Dropping his clothes into the washer, you try to recall what color shirt he was wearing, which pair of boots, and your mind draws a blank. Not much was said over toast and coffee. Your heart did not melt at the sight of his thinning blond hair, and you can't say whether his gaze lingered on you. It would be on a day like this, without clues, without touchstones, that he would leave and never come back.

Already the heat is pressing on the house. You part the living room curtains and look at the sky—pale yellow but dark on the horizon. Out there, just above the wheat fields, clouds are building. Just as you imagined.

By now he is at the McKeevers'. Grace has brought him a cup of coffee, and he is talking with her as he nails up paneling. He cannot see her admiring his backside or unbuttoning her blouse to show more cleavage. Like most women in town, Grace has a crush on Tad. She can't get past those tropical blue eyes, the clean cut of his jaw, the slow, deep smile he offers to not just everyone.

People talk about the pitfalls of marrying a gorgeous woman, but less is said about gorgeous husbands. This was not an issue a few years ago, when your thighs were tight and your skin was flawless, but now that age has begun its slow ambush, you wonder what he's up to. You see him putting down his hammer, reaching for something else. It doesn't help that his work takes him into other people's houses, usually when the mister is gone.

You go into the bedroom, take off your nightgown, and stand before the full-length mirror. Because of the heat, your long auburn hair is pinned up. To hide the strands of gray, you are using a rinse that has just a bit more red than your real color.

Those lines on your forehead—when had they arrived? Eyes, not quite so blue anymore. Lips, definitely thinner. Your breasts haven't fallen, but your hips, passed down like a sentence from your mother and her mother, have always been too wide. While there are plenty of mornings you resent this body, today you feel sorry for it. Slowly, respectfully, you pull on your clothes.

Washing the breakfast dishes, you keep edging looks at the sky. The clouds are coming closer, mushrooming upward; the crows have left the cottonwoods. Under the dense mantle of air everything seems to be waiting. The Strommes' weathervane, a black rooster, spins uncertainly.

Carefully you dry each dish, wipe the table, sweep the floor. "Lady" is playing on the radio. You try to sing a few lines and stop.

Over at the McKeevers', Tad is listening to his scanner. You know he could bolt at any moment. Grace knows this, too; everyone does. Last week—the hottest on record—he lost two days chasing storms.

Sometimes he takes off without a word, pursuing whatever clouds caught his eye. Or he gets a call from a spotter and, just like that, he's gone, barreling down the highway, crossing state lines willy-nilly. Most of these chases are a bust. The storm peters out, or he runs out of road, or the police, trying to keep the foolhardy safe, stop him with their barriers.

Storm chasing is not a harmless sport. It's not a sport at all. It's wasted gas and mud-stuck tires and blown transmissions; it's windshields cracked by hail and radios struck by lightning; it's chores undone and dinners gone cold.

You have told him that he's crazy, that he'll get himself killed. You have cited the damage done to the truck, the cost of all those repairs. You have begged and scolded, threatened divorce, but by now it's clear you're not leaving this place—not, that is, until you're a widow.

Cool air from the fridge chills the sweat on your neck and shoulders. Already it is ninety-two. Again you visit those tall pine trees, that cool mountain lake in your mind. If it weren't for Tad, you would have left Oklahoma a long time ago.

Just once you'd like to live through a spring without knocking on wood. Not that you haven't been lucky. You haven't lost anything that couldn't be replaced, and though your husband doesn't make much money, at least he's handy—not like the car dealers and insurance salesmen your friends are married to. A man should know how to fix things, especially in a place like this.

~

When the rain starts, you straighten up from dusting the coffee table and walk over to the screen door. *Punk ... punk ... punk-punk*—the slow, fat drops strike the road, sending up puffs of dirt. A lone crow streaks above the wheat. You have no idea what birds do in bad weather—whether they fly ahead of it or hunker in barns and silos.

A large grasshopper lands on the screen. Its straw-colored belly, inches from your face, looks like a tiny puzzle. The feet, dainty hooks, grip the wires; the twin antennae twitch faintly.

Strands of your hair lift on their own.

~

Tad must hear the rain, too. You picture him stepping down from the ladder and walking over to Grace's front door. He will sniff the air. His stomach will tighten.

"Looking for Love" is playing on the radio when the announcer breaks in. A long line of storms is moving in from the east. Four counties are under tornado watch.

You sit down on the edge of the sofa, stare at the glossy gray blank of the television screen. Your bare feet are pressed into the carpet Tad installed last month—gold shag, something you'd wanted for ages. Your neighbors don't trade up like this. Leaky roofs, sagging steps—that's about all they dare to replace. They want to keep a low profile, show God how little they require. Understanding this, you fight back.

~

The rain falls harder, bending the wheat, filling the road with puddles. To the north, the sky is almost black. Every few seconds, lightning flashes.

You picture your husband, already in his truck. He shifts into reverse, bumps and splashes down the drive. The wipers are going full tilt. He gets on the CB, tells Duane where to meet him.

~

In a field near Carmen, two funnels merge into one and pick up a barn. Homes are gone; livestock are dead; a girl and her father are missing.

Tad and Duane will be on Highway 64 now, racing north—Tad hunched forward, searching the sky, and Duane, another hell-bent fool, gesturing wildly, shouting over the wind. They'll barely be able to make out the road as rain beats against the windshield, gushes down the doors. Voices and static crackle over the CB. It's big, someone says. A half-mile wide and headed for Jefferson. Tad knows he should stay off the dirt roads, but he yanks the wheel to the right.

~

No need to worry about the others: Your boy is in Lubbock, and your folks had the sense to move away, to a retirement community in Houston. Right now they'll be in the dining room, quietly eating the food on their trays. Tad's parents, who stayed loyal to Enid but take no chances, will already be in their storm cellar.

Tornadoes can change direction. This one could whip around and plow toward Enid. You don't move, not even when they turn on the sirens. There is no point in taking cover, no reason to get the strongbox and head for the cellar. It is not your house you will lose today.

~

You imagine Tad flooring the gas pedal, the tires flinging mud on the doors and windows. Wind is pummeling the hickory trees. Splintered branches and yellow road signs whirl through the blue-black sky. Chunks of hail pound the hood. A ragdoll smacks the windshield.

~

At his funeral, he will be a hero. His father will muster the strength to offer a short eulogy through which his mother will sob. Men will be stone-faced; women will shake their heads and recall his smile and the way he listened when they spoke. One of these women will cover her face with her hands and weep; from this you will draw your own conclusions.

You will move to a state with mountains and water. Gazing at the deep blue lake you have dreamed of all your life, you will think of silos and wheat fields and wind.

~

You see it in your mind's eye: Suddenly it is there, so massive, so near, that all they can see is one brown whirling side. Tad slams into reverse, and the truck's back tires lurch into a gully of mud. He shifts gears, guns the engine; the truck shudders and stays where it is. He reverses, tries again—the tires keep spinning. Duane pushes open the door and jumps out. Tad hollers for him to come back, but Duane just keeps on running through the wheat, his white shirt getting smaller and smaller until it's gone, and there is only the roaring curtain of wind.

~

The tornado expires just south of Pond Creek, leaving three towns flattened and one poor woman wedged in a tree. She is the only confirmed death, but there are lots of injuries, and several people have not been accounted for. Seventeen cows were found along a fence line, electrocuted all at once.

The sky is clear, and the air doesn't feel like warm cotton anymore. You walk out to the porch and sit on the glider. Beyond the puddle-pocked road, the wheat is bent and glistening; above it, swallows dive. The neighbor's bloodhound barks.

Just after suppertime, you see the truck coming down the road, Duane's orange baseball cap, Tad waving out the window. One more time, you get to your feet and wave back.

~

You are lying alongside Tad, your front pressed lightly against his back, your hand resting on his waist. All you can hear are his slow, deep breaths and the constant chirping of crickets.

Sure enough, you think about that spider. You didn't see it fall from the tissue, and you hope it landed safely—that it found, on the glossy contours of a leaf, something to eat, perhaps a mite or two. You hope, when the rain came, that it chanced upon a cozy niche, a place to curl up its legs and rest. Soon enough, it will find another precipice, will wander across the length of the leaf, and cling, bewildered, to the edge of its world.

# Migration

She kept hearing things she wasn't supposed to, information that others had failed to keep secret. The first, the worst, had been the night she'd gotten up to pee and heard her husband in the kitchen. He was on his cell phone, his back to her, and what she heard him whisper was this: "I get hard just talking to you." Carl was reserved, not given to declarations of any sort, or so she had always believed. Not in their most passionate moments had he ever uttered such things.

A few weeks later, browsing titles in the video store, she recognized a voice coming from the next aisle. It was Nora, her longtime friend, godmother of her son. "I know I should invite Erica," Nora was saying, "but honestly, I don't think I can listen to her all evening. You know how much she talks, and always about Carl."

So. When she was laying bare her soul, sharing her hurt and outrage, serving up Carl's failings for her friends to feast on, she was really boring them stiff.

And then, when she was cutting roses one day behind the laurel hedge, her son came out onto the patio with one of his friends. "Yeah, my mom does that, too," Bryan said. "She's always talking shit about my dad. She needs to get over it."

~

They'd been seeing each other for nearly a year, Carl told her. They were serious.

"I wasn't looking," he said. "It just happened."

Erica folded her arms and leaned back against the dresser. "Where did it 'just happen' to happen?"

He tucked another pair of socks into his suitcase. "She's a patient."

The answer was a clue, and her mind raced to fill in the picture. Carl was a cosmetic dentist. At what point did the attraction occur? Did he fall in love with her mouth? Or was it her breasts, just a few inches below, that caught his eye? Did he kiss her when she was in the chair? *Did they do it in the chair?*

"What's her name? I can ask that, right?"

"Alexis." He paused, as if assessing the risk. "Harrington."

Erica arched an eyebrow. "Classy name for a tramp."

Carl, ignoring this, zipped up his suitcase. Erica regarded his bald spot, bigger now. She had seen him in the bathroom, trying to view the top of his head with a hand mirror—how he hated losing his russet locks. Maybe she was rid of him just in time. Let the tramp deal with his hypertension and carpal tunnel and enlarged prostate.

"A *year*, Carl? When were you planning on telling me?"

He sighed, shook his head. "All along."

She must still love him, she realized. Somewhere, under all this loathing, a pointless love must still be alive. "What a coward you are," she murmured.

He walked to the door, his back rigid, and set the suitcase down. "What do you want? We should talk about this ahead of time."

Her eyes swept over the room, taking in the mahogany sleigh bed, the antique armoire, the bay window, and the tennis court beyond.

"I'm so glad you're not poor," she said, smiling.

~

While their lawyers managed the paperwork, Erica stayed in the house, and Carl took an apartment near his office. It was a straightforward divorce with obvious solutions. Carl, the guilty breadwinner, would pay both child support and alimony (she was a licensed real estate broker, but sales had slowed in recent years). He would get the Jaguar; she would have the Range Rover. He would keep the Mill Valley home, where his practice was, where Bryan's school was, and Erica would acquire the house at Lake Tahoe, where she would move. She was the one with the freedom, so much of it, so suddenly.

Anyway, she preferred their vacation home and had often fantasized about living in the mountains year round, one honest season at a time. She was not keen on seeing her friends any time soon, or her hair stylist, or her banker, or the postman, or anyone else in this chatty little town. No, she didn't mind leaving Mill Valley, except for Bryan. She would miss her son terribly. Bryan was a senior this year; naturally, he didn't want to change high schools.

"Will you be okay," Erica asked him, "living with your father?"

He frowned at the magazine he was reading. "Why shouldn't I be?"

"Oh, I don't know … his social life."

Bryan looked up at her. "You mean his girlfriend? I've met her, Mom. She isn't awful."

Erica stared at her son.

"It's not a big deal," he said. "Tahoe isn't that far away. I'll be up there skiing in a couple months." He turned back to his magazine. "Everything's *fine*."

She bent down and gave him a hug, told him to call her anytime he wanted, even if it was late. Then she kissed his forehead and left the room. Maybe he was trying to be strong. Maybe he *was* strong. The truth was, he had broken her heart.

~

The rooms were hushed and clean, as if they'd been waiting for her, as if her arrival was expected. She stood in the hallway, breathing in the familiar, restorative scents: cedar, pine, a trace of wood smoke. The house was hers now, Erica reflected with slow amazement. This time she would not be leaving. She set down her purse, dropped the keys on the hall table. They would take care of each other, she and this house.

Erica crossed the living room and paused at the window, beyond which she could see a bright blue patch of lake framed by tall conifers. Just a few feet from the window stood a massive redwood. Two shiny black carpenter ants raced across its coarse, fissured bark. A mountain jay flashed from a branch, and the sudden movement startled her.

The house had been built on high ground a couple miles from Lake Tahoe's west shore. There were only a handful of homes up here and plenty of privacy between them. Below the deck, the property sloped toward a pine forest studded with twisting manzanita. The front of the house faced a marshy area, and Erica walked back across the thick rug and stood in the doorway studying the wet expanse, which contained, at the moment, several dozen Canada geese. Erica watched their movements, nonchalant and avid at once, as they roamed the wet pockets, searching for whatever sodden herbage geese ate. Grasping with their bills, they jerked their heads to tear the plants free. She studied their robust beauty: the solid breadth of their bodies, the sturdy legs and flat feet, the long black necks and white cheeks. If there were any gender differences, she could not detect them.

After unpacking the Range Rover and putting away her clothes and papers, Erica poured herself a glass of pinot grigio and set her dinner on the granite breakfast bar beneath the window. From here she could study the marsh and, beyond that, the ridges of blue mountains that changed hues throughout the day. Tucked behind the pines to the left was where Tom, the caretaker, lived. Off to the right and also out of view was the Sangers' place, which belonged to John Sanger and his daughter, Lexi—Erica wasn't sure where the mother wound up. Lexi, who was somewhere in her thirties, was "not right," and when she was on the porch she could sometimes be heard talking to herself, a gentle and insistent scolding.

The geese had stopped eating. Plump, dark shapes in the fading light, some were standing; others hunkered close to the ground. Erica forked up some salad and peered at them. What patience they had, to stand or sit through the long night, a chill wind lifting the tips of their feathers. Maybe it was something deeper than patience, some primal, unassailable power. Maybe what these birds possessed was simply the ability to abide, to hold from birth their place in this world.

After dinner Erica washed and dried the few dishes and set up the coffee maker for the next morning. Before shutting off the lights, she paused to admire the travertine tiles and cherry cabinets, the wrought iron pulls in the shape of twigs. They had remodeled the kitchen a couple years ago, and at this point there was nothing about the property she would change. Heat was lost, she knew, in the high ceilings, but how nice it was to lie on the sofa or either of the beds and look up into the treetops. Everything about the house soothed her—the cedar walls, the hand-hewn beams, the large, smooth stones around the fireplace. Again she was struck with the feeling that the house was offering itself to her, that she had walked in right on cue.

Tired from the long day, Erica undressed and got ready for bed. She was not unused to being here without Carl; when he couldn't break away from the office, she and Bryan had often come up a few days ahead of him. Staying here alone gave her no misgivings—Tom was nearby, and the house was equipped with a sophisticated alarm system.

She slipped into bed and turned off the lamp, and for several moments she lay without moving, letting her body warm the sheets. With all the windows closed, the house was utterly quiet. Through the tall windows above her, she could see black branches and cold, bright stars. She thought of the geese, huddled out there in the open marsh. Right where they belonged.

~

The next morning Erica stood before the living room window sipping coffee and watching a fat gray squirrel who was likewise watching her. He was sitting on the deck railing, gnawing on a large seed and studying her with mild interest—at least he *seemed* to be studying her: that shining black eye did not blink or waver, even when she wiggled a finger at him. The window might have been his television and she the show: the female human inside her shelter. In any case, he seemed perfectly calm, spinning that seed in his quick paws, scrupulously chewing each bite. Certain, that's how he looked—absolutely sure of himself.

Just like the woman at the DMV, Erica thought. She was someone you didn't forget—every bit of seventy, wearing a red cowboy hat and red boots, her jeans tucked into them; fierce blue eyes; savage tan; long white braid down her back. They were standing in line and, noting the NAME CHANGE form in Erica's hand, she said with a smile, "Getting married?"

Erica shook her head. "Divorced. Changing back to my maiden name."

"You like that name?" the woman asked.

"Not really. It's Vreuls. People can't spell it or say it."

The woman shrugged. "Change it to something else."

Erica blinked at her. "You can do that?"

"Sure, honey! I've done it *three* times—no man involved. You can get sick of a name"—she tapped the form in Erica's hand and grinned—"just like you can get sick of a man."

"But how do you decide? I'd have no idea what to call myself."

"Honey, look at Prince, look at Queen Latifah." She laughed, her gold dental work gleaming. "You can call yourself Wonder Woman if you want to." She turned away then and over her shoulder added, "You don't have to worry yourself to death over it. It's just a name."

And right there in line Erica started to ponder her options. Something from nature would be nice, she thought. Erica Mountain—no. Erica Snow—better, not great. Erica Stream? That one made her think of urine. Rivers? Too many r's. Sun? Moon? Too Asian. Sky—too new agey. Star—no. Maybe a kind of tree—Cedar? Didn't sound right. Erica Pine? That made her think of pining away. Erica Oak. Too many vowels ... Lake? A lake was calming, curative. A fresh start. That's who she would be: Erica Lake.

Understandably, her father wasn't pleased with this change. When she told him, over coffee at his home in Berkeley, he looked at the floor and shook his head, as if this were just another in a series of undue punishments he'd been handed (Erica's mother had died a couple years earlier, his financial adviser was under investigation, and the previous week his parked car had been totaled by a drunk driver).

"Dad," she said, putting her hand on his arm. "It's just something I needed to do. Don't take it personally."

He jerked his head back up and glared at her. "It's my goddamn name you got rid of—how am I supposed to take it? Jesus. I had no idea you hated your name."

"I don't hate it."

"Then why did you change it?"

Erica gave him a small, helpless smile. "I don't know, Dad. It was sort of sudden."

He gave a disgusted hiss, rolled his watery blue eyes. "That's great. Glad you gave it some thought."

Carl had not seemed surprised, or at least he hadn't shown it. She had called him with the news. There was the briefest pause before he replied. "You're still who you are, Erica, no matter what you're calling yourself." His tone was sarcastic, and she ignored the implication. It was just like him to criticize her in this oblique, cowardly manner.

Bryan, on the other hand, had accepted her name change without rancor. It could be that he voiced other feelings at school, but when she told him he had only shrugged, in that bored teenage fashion, and said, "Whatever," as if the topic could not be less significant, to him or anyone.

Not a single person had said anything nice about her new name, and the more she thought about it, the more vexed she became. A few words of cheer—what would it cost them? Changing one's name was no small thing—oddly easy, but no small thing. It was like making a high dive: You had to get your nerve up, and afterward it felt wonderful.

Her toast popped up, and Erica walked back into the kitchen. She spread the margarine carefully, covering the entire slice. She was trying to go slowly, to become more aware of what she was doing and catch herself before she blundered into old habits. Erica

Lake, she'd decided, deserved a fair chance.

Carl was wrong. With practice, people could change. Wasn't it just a matter of seeing what was wrong, or lacking, and making adjustments? If she had bored her friends, annoyed her son, from now on she wouldn't. Perhaps there were things—quirks or mannerisms—that could not be expunged, but how hard could it be to keep her smart mouth shut?

Eating her toast at the breakfast bar, Erica watched the geese browse. She pictured their broad, rubbery feet breaking through the thin layers of ice as they roved the marsh—the nights were already cold. Where would they go, she wondered, when the snow came? She had read that many Canada geese were no longer bothering to migrate, particularly those in populated areas. The margins between people and wildlife were beginning to blur, and there was something unnerving about the intersection: pigeons living on dropped French fries; raptors nesting on sooty skyscrapers; geese, sated and lazy, staggering through city parks. How many generations would pass before their wings grew stunted and useless? *Fly*, she thought, staring at the flock. *Fly before it's too late.*

After breakfast Erica cleaned up, then put on a jacket and went outside. The cold air took her breath away. There were patches of ice on the front steps and hardened puddles on the road. The pine trees stood sharply against the adamant blue sky. There was a figure in the distance; from the girth and the wide-brimmed hat, Erica recognized Maria Blattner, who said very little to anyone and devoted most of her time to watching birds.

The geese, honking, retreated as she approached. Some resumed their feeding but kept a nervous eye on her; a few groomed themselves in a show of indifference, running their beaks down their buff-colored breasts. Erica stood at the edge of the marsh, arms folded, and watched them carry on. One especially large bird kept menacing the rest, lowering his head and running forward, claiming whatever turf he pleased. The others moved off, made room around him, seeming to accept his behavior in the same way that people sharing a holiday dinner might tolerate a cantankerous grandfather.

"Hello there!" Tom crossed his yard and walked up to her. "Got your letter," he said, nodding. "Good to see you." He smiled at her, and the wrinkles around his eyes deepened. He was wearing jeans and an old canvas jacket that didn't look warm enough. His brown hair, threaded with silver now, curled over his collar and tufted over his ears. He looked thinner than he had in July.

Erica stepped forward and gave him a hug. "Good morning."

"Got everything you need?" he asked.

"I'm fine. The place looks great."

"We had a black bear up here last week. She behaved herself, though." He looked over at the geese. "Never seen so many of them here."

"When do they migrate?"

"Soon as they get cold enough, I guess," he said, bringing his kind gaze back to her. She had never met anyone like Tom. In his hands, in the way he spoke and moved, there was a gentleness, a steady forgiveness. How he managed this mercy she had no idea. His wife had died, much too slowly, of bone cancer, and not long after that his son was killed in a highway accident—a truck filled with landscape boulders lost its load. Where did you lay that kind of grief? What sort of bargain had he made with himself in order to continue?

"I'm going into town"—he smiled self-consciously—"for a haircut. I'll be going to the hardware store, too. You need anything?"

Erica shook her head. "No, thanks, I'm fine for now."

"Okay, then. You have a good day." He walked over to his truck and opened the door. "Oh. They got that Internet up here now if you want it."

She had not even brought her laptop, and while she did have a cell phone, she never used it for anything but phone calls, something that baffled her son.

"Thanks, but I'm going to try and manage without it."

Tom nodded and swung himself into the cab. Predictably, he didn't ask her about Carl, nor would he. He knew from her letter that they were divorced, and for him that was sufficient information. Which was just another thing she liked about him.

Watching him drive off, Erica didn't notice the goose who had moved away from the flock and was now walking toward her with short, purposeful steps. Head turned to one side, the bird kept her in view with one dark, glistening eye. Erica smiled at its determined waddle and apparent fearlessness. People must have fed these birds at some point, and clearly this one was looking for another handout.

"For your own good," Erica said, "I am not feeding you." The goose stopped within a yard of her and gave an experimental quack.

"See," Erica said, holding out her hands, "no breads, no seeds, nothing."

The bird remained motionless, and Erica cocked her head at it. "What do you want?" Again the goose quacked softly. Erica stooped down and tentatively extended her hand; geese were mean, and she didn't want this one chomping her finger. But instead of striking at her, the bird became submissive, ducking its head and taking a slow step forward. Erica touched its supple neck. "You're a friendly one, aren't you?"

The bird answered with another throaty sound, and Erica ran her fingertips down the pillowy feathers of its breast.

"I have to go," she murmured, getting to her feet. "My hands are freezing. Go back to your buddies." She turned and began walking across the road, and the bird promptly followed her. Erica wheeled around. "Be a good goose and go home." The creature didn't move.

"Suit yourself." She hurried across the road to her house, and the bird, waddling faster, kept coming. "I know you can't do stairs," she said over her shoulder as she ran up the steps, and sure enough the goose stopped at the bottom and eyed the steep rise.

"Go home," Erica urged. The bird opened its huge wings and, just like that, it was standing beside her.

Now what? She certainly didn't want a goose in the house, pooping on the rugs, scattering mites and down. Carefully she opened the door, squeezed in, and turned around. The goose moved its head to keep her in sight as she slowly shut the door. She heard a dispirited quack.

Every few minutes Erica sidled over to the edge of the window and checked; she could see its back half: the tan wing feathers arranged in delicate layers, the tapered black tail and white under-body, the stalwart legs, the webbed, prehistoric feet. The bird stood there for nearly half an hour before ambling back to the marsh.

Which couldn't be normal. She had given it no food, no promise of food. What did it want with her? Could a goose be mentally ill?

Erica had once watched a documentary about an Antarctic expedition. She couldn't recall the name of the film or the precise nature of the mission. What did stay with her, horribly, was a scene in which a penguin, following its own unfathomable imperative, broke away from its group and headed not for water and survival but back to the icy mountains. With instructions not to interfere with the wildlife, the scientists made no attempt to redirect the misguided bird, though they did keep the cameras rolling for several agonizing minutes as the penguin trudged farther and farther into oblivion.

The suicide of a lone penguin might not be significant by itself, but not a month went by now that Erica didn't hear of some aberrant activity in the animal kingdom. Tigers raising pigs, gorillas adopting kittens, dogs befriending elephants. In these doubtful times maybe animals, as rattled as people, were seizing comfort wherever they could.

She couldn't imagine what this bird saw in her that gave it hope.

~

Erica spent the rest of the day organizing her belongings and clearing away Carl's clothes and toiletries, which she stowed in boxes in the garage alongside his skis and fishing tackle. She did this reflexively, not pausing until the job was finished and she was standing before the large framed photograph over the sofa. Snow-laced mountains, deep blue water. Carl, sitting behind the wheel of his newly purchased Chris-Craft, Erica in the other seat, Bryan standing between them. Bright smiles all around.

The picture had to go, not so much for the pain it triggered but because it was a misrepresentation, no longer accurate. Had it been accurate even then? Given the timeline Carl had confessed to, Alexis should be there, too, standing stubbornly behind Carl, her hands clutching the back of his seat. Erica wished she'd been smart enough not to ask "How long?" One after another, her recollections had turned suspect: last winter, for instance, when Carl returned from a conference and scarcely had his coat off before he was steering Erica into the bedroom. At the time she'd been flattered by his need; now she assumed that Alexis had primed the pump and the conference had been a lie.

In one swift movement, Erica lifted the photo from the wall and slid it behind the sofa. Hurling the picture off the deck would have been fun, but there was Bryan to consider.

Twenty-one years of matrimony. Why wasn't she slogging around the house in her bathrobe, pockets overflowing with Kleenex? There had been a few weepy days early on, a couple times when she wanted to give Carl a good whack, send Alexis a cute little coral snake, but these urges had dried up surprisingly soon.

She could not, after all, blame him forever. He had fallen out of love with her—was that even a punishable offense? The fact that he had lied about it for so long was shameful but drearily commonplace: He was spineless, unexceptional. Could he help that? Her outrage was gone, she realized, and what she felt for him now was indistinct: neither forgiveness nor indifference but something in between.

Maybe the name change had helped. Erica remembered how exhilarated she had felt when she left the DMV, as if she possessed a fabulous secret, as if everything were suddenly clarified and life, unveiled at last, really was that simple. You could slip on a new name like you could slip on a stunning new outfit, and from there the journey was boundless. What was there to any of us? Thoughts, feelings, likes, dislikes, fears, urges, and all of them constantly slipping and shifting. *This* amounted to a personality, this reckless, colliding assortment—amazing that people had enough conviction to haul themselves out of bed.

You didn't need a lot to get through life—luck, reflexes, decent genes. Wisdom was an option. You could live to be ninety without paying much attention, with no end to what you could miss on the way.

Once, when she was washing dishes, Bryan, who was sitting at the table, said, "Change the tune, Mom."

Erica turned around. "What tune?"

"Whatever that song is—you've been humming it over and over."

"Really? I didn't realize I was humming."

"Mom. You hum all the time." He looked up from his book. "It's okay. It means you're happy, right? Only sometimes it gets, you know, annoying."

How could a person hum and not know it? And why *did* she

hum? Was she happy? Christ—who knew if they were happy?

Maybe she hummed to calm herself. Maybe humming was a remedy, like rocking. Or was it more like a tic, more the problem than the solution?

In any case, learning about this embarrassing habit had given her pause, similar to the way she felt after Nora's Oscar party a couple years ago. There were eight of them at the dinner table, good friends chatting amiably. Erica poured herself a third glass of wine and began talking about the new outdoor grill they'd bought, how Carl had put it together wrong, and how he kept insisting that he'd done it right, even after he couldn't get the damn thing lit, and it was the *paper boy* who noticed that the grills were upside down. She thought it was a pretty good story; Carl did not.

"Your stories are all the same," he said later that night. "Mocking." She was lounging on the bed, and he glowered at her in the mirror. "You're not near as clever as you think you are." Drunk as she was, the remark lodged deep. She suspected it was true.

Well. If she were going to change her habits, this was the place to start. Alone in these rooms she could probably catch herself humming. As for her stories, who, aside from the occasional goose, would she tell them to?

~

The sky was cloudy the next morning, the air less chilly than the day before. Erica breathed deeply, took in the complicated mix of autumn odors: damp bark, pine needles, wet leaves, chimney smoke. At the edge of the yard a brown squirrel spiraled madly up and down a cedar tree; jays quarreled in the branches above. Out in the marsh several geese, honking softly, swam across a pool of water. Others, clustered on a grassy mound close to the road, were still resting, their heads tucked backward, their bills buried in their wings.

Erica heard a familiar voice. She walked down to the edge of the Sangers' property and stopped behind a cluster of young pines. Through the lime-green branches she could see Lexi sitting on her porch, her long dark hair tangled around her face. She was wearing boots and a heavy coat over what looked to be a yellow nightgown. "No, I don't think so," she murmured. "Not today … You don't need that … We'll discuss it later … No, I don't think so … You want to go where?" There was a brief pause between sentences as if she were reading from a script. Her tone suggested a parental role—the absent mother? Erica wondered if Lexi "heard" the other character in her head or if she was just stringing along a series of random comments.

Erica stepped from behind the pines and approached the Sangers' front yard. "Hello, Lexi," she called out.

Lexi stopped speaking and stared wide-eyed at Erica; abruptly she bent forward over her lap. Sometimes you could get a hi out of her. "See you later!" Erica said, waving at the top of Lexi's head.

Careful not to disturb the resting birds, Erica walked around to the side of the marsh where several geese were busy sawing off tall stalks of grass. An especially large goose, catching sight of her, flapped its wings and honked loudly, and the nearby birds moved deeper into the wetland. But one of the snoozing geese roused itself and began to approach her, presumably the same one that followed her yesterday—aside from variations in size, they all looked identical. Erica smiled at the jaunty white cheeks. God must love those chinstraps, she thought, to make them so perfectly, again and again.

"Hello," she said. The goose eyed her thoroughly, turning its head this way and that. She squatted, and the goose marched right over, nudged her hand with its glossy bill. She stroked its supple neck, the cool sleeve of black feathers sliding beneath her fingertips.

"What are you, anyway? A goose or a gander?" She tilted her head at the goose. "Quack twice if you're a girl."

The bird fixed her in its gaze and gave two low quacks.

"I knew it!" Erica said. "I had a feeling." She drew her palm over the springy arrangement of wing feathers—to touch the back of a wild goose! "Do you know how lovely you are?"

Again the bird followed her across the road and all the way to her door. This time Erica walked into the house and kept the door open behind her to see if the creature would be bold enough to venture inside. The goose moved its long neck around, assessing the situation from many angles, then stepped across the threshold. Erica came around and gently pushed the door shut, and the goose looked up at her face.

"A lot warmer in here, right?" She walked down the hall to the kitchen, pulled out a chair at the table, and sat down. Which was all, evidently, the bird required, just to be with her, wherever she was, for as long as possible. Twice it followed her into the bathroom, once into the bedroom, and the rest of the time it settled beside whatever chair she sat in. Respectfully the bird stayed off the furniture, and its two minor indiscretions were confined to the kitchen floor.

After what seemed like a sufficient amount of bonding time, Erica went out onto the porch, and of course the goose followed. There was nothing she could do but give it the slip and so she opened the door just wide enough to squeeze back inside. "Bye now," she said, shutting the door as tactfully as possible. The bird, no doubt hungry, stayed only a couple minutes this time before joining the others.

Erica watched from the window as the goose walked back to the marsh and immediately began feeding. So. A goose could become smitten with a person. Why her, though? Why not Tom? Twice now she had seen Tom standing alone at the edge of the marsh. Wasn't he far more worthy of admiration? Or Maria Blattner, who was always traipsing the marsh, who loved birds more than anything? Or Lexi, who spent so much time on her porch, locked in her strange world—surely she could use a feathered friend. But the goose had chosen Erica. Erica Lake. A person you couldn't even count on yet. She wanted to see this infatuation as a compliment, evidence of her value, but how much credit could you give a goose?

~

The next morning Erica turned on her cell phone and was about to call Bryan when she received a text message from him: U OK? Three letters from which to draw any number of conclusions: that he missed her? that he was concerned? that he was in a rush? that he wanted to talk? that he didn't? She was certain of this last possibility. On the rare occasions that his phone rang, he ignored it; she wasn't even sure that he bothered listening to his voice mail. Soon even the clever abbreviations he and his friends used would become too bothersome, and the English language would devolve into symbols, cyber hieroglyphics that only the young would be able to decode. A culture that was stripping itself of language, refusing even the mildest degrees of accountability—Erica couldn't conceive the consequences.

At least he had contacted her—that was something. Her impulse was to call him, to ask how he was, to tell him about the goose, the new Internet access, her plans to start selling real estate in the spring; most of all, she wanted to show him that she could carry on a whole conversation without once criticizing his father.

She would call him this weekend—she needed to—but for now she would speak *his* language. Erica opened the message window and punched in a reply: Gr8 & U? There was, to be honest, some fun involved.

When Erica stepped outside, the goose was already on the porch, ready for anything.

"Let's take a walk," she said, and they did—that day and the next day and each day after. They walked down the side of the road, past the Sangers' house, past the Blattners' faux Swiss chalet, past the jammed-up beaver pond, past the listing red barn, past more pine woods and another small marsh, past the climbing black bear someone carved from a cedar stump, all the way to the main road that led down to the lake. And as they walked, the goose looked around, quacking companionably here and there as if commenting on the scenery.

Today, passing the beaver pond, Erica regarded the great mound of sticks and weeds. She hoped to see the beavers themselves, nosing along the water's surface, but she hadn't yet. Had they moved off, or were they tucked away in their lodge, their furry closeness keeping them warm?

She thought about the winter ahead, the snow that would pile up to the window sills, maybe higher. One year they came up for Christmas and got trapped—fifteen feet of snow in five days. Three plows broke down trying to clear this road.

Well, she would stock up, think ahead, use all five senses. She would spend the long winter next to the fire, and she would read about this world. Last night she had found a book in the living room, full of gorgeous photos, about animals and what they do to stay alive. The privation, the *commitment*. She couldn't remember buying the book, and she certainly had not read it—how long had these creatures sat on this shelf, their beauty and struggles ignored? The least she could do was learn their names.

Snow was on the way, Tom said, a foot or more by the end of the week. Erica looked down at the goose walking calmly alongside her. She wanted to offer some warning, a head's up, but she supposed that in its hollow bones, the bird already knew, would always be ready.

There were countless mysteries, observed or missed, unfolding every instant. In this tiny pocket of the universe, a goose had a crush on her—she could live with that. And when the snows came and her bird flew away, she would live with that, too.

# Looks for Life

Never underestimate the things that money can buy. Obtain the right people, give them enough money, and prepare yourself for a miracle.

In Alex's case, two miracles were involved: the one that saved her life and the one that saved her face. Well, they didn't actually *save* her face; they built her a new one. Apart from the healing, nature had nothing to do with the face that Alex brought home from the hospital.

Eighteen months ago, on a warm September morning, Alex was driving her red MG along the Marin County coastline. I never liked that car; it spent more time in the shop than on the road, and what did we need with a third car anyway? But the biggest drawback, I complained, was the size: Something that slight was dangerous. Alex, who had spent a good deal of her glorious youth in that car, paid me no heed. Whatever Alex disagreed with she sweetly ignored, a habit that infuriated me. I can't tell you how many times I stood waiting for a response that never came.

On a steep switchback in the redwoods, not far from Stinson

Beach, Alex was sideswiped by four young men in a Jeep. By the time I learned of the accident, she was undergoing surgery at San Francisco General. Broken collarbone, cracked pelvis, broken tibia, crushed ankle, collapsed lung, punctured kidney, ruptured spleen, and broken nose, jaw, and cheekbone. At some point the doctor's voice fell away, and there was only a roaring in my ears.

As soon as Alex was stabilized, her parents had her air-lifted to Stanford University Medical Center. For me they arranged accommodations at a nearby hotel, where I stayed for most of the ninety-one days it took various gifted surgeons to save Alex's life. While she might have survived her injuries in another trauma center, the restorations would not have been as graceful, nor would she have been walking again so soon.

Her face, though: That's where the real talent took over. Alex's father is the president of a rental car company; her mother is the principal shareholder of the world's third-largest cosmetics firm. I don't know how or where they looked, but a prodigy was procured. A man known by one name: Malik.

Only in a rare light, at a singular angle, can you see any trace of his work. That's because he did everything from inside her nose or her mouth, or at her hairline. No scars was the whole point. And you would not believe what can be done these days with artificial bone and skin.

He could have matched the side of her face that wasn't smashed up; he did give her that option. No, Alex told him; she wanted something new. A chin out of a book. A nose that had never been. This, of course, pleased him. Plastic surgeons don't want to replicate; they want to invent—they want to pull back the curtain and take your breath away. Eight surgeries later, he did just that.

Her parents wanted to sue; her sisters cried. I tried to speak but couldn't.

She is beautiful—who would dispute it? Attractive before, she is magnificent now.

~

In the first few weeks after Alex came home, I would often find her in the bathroom, studying her reflection as if she were trying to understand it. She would turn this way, that way, then stare at herself straight on. After forty-one years she was meeting a different person in the mirror; the adjustment could not have been easy. Even though Malik had given her the face she wanted, I wondered if she ever mourned her lost image, if she were ever sorry. I couldn't ask her that.

In bed, looking down the length of her slim body, it was hard to imagine the injuries she had suffered. After the other surgeons were done, Malik performed his laser magic on her scars, all but erasing them. Only minute, silvery lines remained: at her ankle, along her shin, etched on her lower back. She had lost some weight; otherwise, this was the body I had adored for thirteen years, and I couldn't stop marveling over the fact that she was here. Whole and safe.

When I looked at her face, which could still startle me, it was her eyes that gave me comfort. A soft and steady brown, her eyes had not changed: Alex was there.

In our early days, when love eclipsed everything else, when just the sight of her jacket on a chair made my heart quicken, when all we asked of life was the chance to be together, we would spend long afternoons lying in bed, gazing at each other's faces. Alex had a sensual face: broad forehead, strong jaw. Her nose was rounded at the tip; her lips were wide and full and inviting. She had laugh lines around her eyes, which I thought made her even more alluring, and all year long her skin had a ruddy glow; she looked healthy, animate—a skier just off the slopes.

Now the tan was gone, her new skin was flawless, and each of her features was trimmed down: the forehead narrowed, the chin chiseled, the nose tapered. Her mouth was utterly changed, the once lavish lips replaced with a more demure pair. *Why had he changed her lips?*

Well, it's a lot to ask, isn't it? When I fell for Alex, I fell for her face—the original one. Suddenly I was supposed to love the face of a stranger—and a younger one, at that. During the final surgery, Malik couldn't resist a nip and a tuck around her eyes; Alex looked like a thirty-year-old. I was still my staid forty-three.

It wasn't as if we could take up where we left off. She was a phenom, a triumph; frankly, I was in awe of her. Much of the time I didn't know what to say, how to proceed. I gave her room, made small talk, pretended. We both did.

I did break down once in front of her; I couldn't help it. We were sitting at the kitchen table discussing a menu for dinner, and suddenly I wanted—*needed*—to see Alex the way she was. It was like missing a close friend who has passed away, the agitation that comes with remembering she is gone. So keenly did I miss Alex's face—the real one, the one somewhere underneath—that I started to cry. Alex rose from her chair, wrapped her arms around me, and murmured that everything was going to be okay, that she was the same, that really she hadn't changed at all. "I love you," she whispered. "I love you." At that point, she still did.

Change is an odd thing. It's with us all the time, yet we can't feel it, can't gauge it, until afterward. I don't know how many weeks had passed before it occurred to me that I hadn't heard Alex laugh, not in the endearing way she used to. Alex had a laugh like no one else. For a couple seconds she would just stare at the person speaking, as if absorbing the full force of whatever had amused her, and then she would let out a single, startling whoop. Now, her laugh—which wasn't frequent, come to think of it—was more of a chuckle. When I mentioned it to her, casually, carefully, she looked puzzled and said, "Really? My laugh is different?" I don't think she had any idea that she was changing by the minute, growing into another version of herself, the one her doctors had set in motion.

~

The season was in full swing now, and Dana and I could barely keep up with the orders. Hidden Cottage Herbs was outgrowing its greenhouses; it was time to start looking for a second facility, maybe even a partnership.

"I found another van," Dana said. "Great price. Thirty-four thousand miles. The racks are already in it."

"Where is it?"

"Millbrae, but they'll drive it up here. They're bedding growers— *were* bedding growers."

"We'll need another driver," I said.

Dana looked up from the flat of garlic chives she was trimming. Sun from the skylight shone down on her straight blonde hair; she always wore it parted in the middle, bangs across her eyebrows. Her eyes widened. "How about Garret?"

Garret was Dana's brother, and I liked him a lot. He was handsome, boyish, disarmingly good-natured. Men and women alike fell hard for Garret, not understanding that he was indiscriminately charming. Garret had helped us out on a few occasions, and I knew he could win over even the edgiest customer. The problem was, it was Garret who made them edgy, usually by showing up late. He had no sense of schedule or urgency, and if he spotted something en route that intrigued him, he was apt to drift off course.

"Maybe." I sighed. "We'll see." I poked another four seeds into a pot and looked up. "Ricky wants more hours." Ricky was our go-to guy, the one we depended on to do everything from deliveries to van repairs to irrigation maintenance.

Dana shook her head. "He's already working ten-hour days. He's getting expensive."

She was right; we had to watch the overtime. I finished seeding the basil and reached for a bag of marjoram seeds. "Is it worth it?" I asked. "Expanding?"

Dana shrugged. "If we can find a partner, it might be easier." She plucked another chive plant from the flat and neatly shaped it with four quick snips. It was her favorite job here; she loved the smell of fresh garlic, how it lingered for hours on her hands and clothes. "How's Alex doing? Is she back at the shop yet?"

Alex owned a hat store in north Berkeley, not far from our house. Business was good, no matter what time of year, and most of that success stemmed from Alex and her knack for putting people at ease. For one thing, she wore hats herself. She used to say that the hat she selected each morning dictated the sort of day she would have: A cowboy hat granted confidence, a cloche brought out playfulness, a beret bestowed tenderness, a newsboy cap gave her daring. There was no quicker way to break out of a mold, she believed, than by jamming on a hat. People entered her store, game but tentative, and strode out happily, bold new versions of themselves. They'd look at the glossy photos on the walls—gorgeous celebrities in audacious headgear—and they'd see Alex, laughing with other customers, handing them Panamas and Trilbys, moving to the beat of the Caribbean music she played, and in no time at all they, too, would be trying on fresh looks, smiling at themselves in the mirrors.

"Actually," I said, "she's selling her lease."

Dana looked up, her scissors in mid-snip. "What?"

"It's true. She's tired of hats. She doesn't even wear them anymore."

"Wow. What's she going to do?"

"I don't know. She wants to get stronger, I know that. She's joined a gym, and she's hired this trainer who specializes in injury rehab."

"Does she still have a lot of pain?"

"Only in her leg. Her back is pretty good now." I stood up and stretched, groaning. "Speaking of backs."

Dana nodded. "All this bending over." She slid the last flat of chives onto the rack and wiped off her scissors. "Something I've been wondering. How is it between you two these days?"

I looked over at her.

"Yeah," Dana said. "That."

"It's okay," I said, sitting back down. "Fine." Dana was my closest friend and the only person I knew who would ask me a question like that.

"Because the other day I was thinking about it. I was thinking how it must be sort of like sleeping with another woman, you know? I mean, it's Alex, but with a hot new look." She grinned. "Like getting your cake and eating it, too."

"You'd think." I twisted the tie on the marjoram seeds and tucked them back in the drawer. "It's hard, Dana. It's going to take time."

"Well, yeah, I get that. It was a shock for all of us."

"She doesn't look like Alex," I said. "How am I supposed to be okay with that?"

Dana looked at me steadily. "I don't know, but you're going to have to figure it out. You can't just keep wishing for the old Alex. You're still in love, right?"

"Of course."

"Shelley, the thing is, Alex didn't break any contracts. It's her face, her life. This new look—it's obviously something she really wanted to do. How long are you going to resist it?"

I didn't answer. Dana had a talent for getting right to the point.

"And you have to remember," she added, "she hasn't changed fundamentally."

I stood up and walked over to the window, beyond which I could see the verdant rows of plants in one of our greenhouses. "I'm not so sure about that," I said. "What about the hat store? What about her laugh? Have *you* heard her laugh since she came home?"

"I guess not," said Dana. "But I haven't been around her that much. She's been through a lot—maybe she just doesn't feel like laughing."

"Maybe," I said, doubtful.

"Shelley," she said, "be in the moment."

~

Dana was right. I resented Alex for wanting to change, for making a decision that was hers to make. If I was unhappy, whose fault was that? When you got right down to it, how much effort had I made on our behalf? I'd just been treading water, hoping day by day to feel less bad.

*Be in the moment* was Dana's mantra. She and her brother seemed to have a gift for this, perhaps a genetic advantage. I kept spinning away, losing sight of the world in front of me, stranding myself in days long gone.

Now I began to regard Alex more closely, more calmly, ignoring the tug of memories. It certainly wasn't hard to look at her—believe me, *everyone* looked at her. And looked. In stores, we got better service; in restaurants, better tables. It was as if her beauty were a kind of currency or luck: People simply wanted to be near her. I felt myself letting go, forgetting sometimes that Alex's face was not God-given. The idea that I could be newly seduced, that I might fall in love all over again, edged into my thoughts.

And I could see that Alex felt it, the change in me, the growing receptiveness. She became more animated, more willing to confide. "I don't miss my old face," she said, "not at all—that clown nose, the big lips." She paused. "But I am nervous about the way I look now. It's a big responsibility." Alex had no false modesty about her appearance. She said it was like being given the keys to a luxury car, one she didn't quite know how to drive.

Beyond brief phone exchanges, usually regarding a financial transaction (Alex had a trust fund), Alex's parents still weren't talking to her. Presumably they had paid Malik for his services, but they were appalled at what he had done to their daughter and considered the transformation a conspiracy: He and Alex had plotted against the family genes with no regard for the feelings of others. While Alex had never had a close relationship with her enterprising parents, I knew that this condemnation bothered her—probably because it roused her guilt—and I resolved to be as supportive as I could. For love and loyalty, she could count on me.

And so things between us began to improve, or so it seemed. Having sold the hat shop, Alex was helping out a couple days a week at the nursery, answering phones, grooming plants; I think she enjoyed it. At home we worked in the yard together, weeding the vegetable beds, staking up the dahlias and delphiniums. We sponged the living room walls a restful Tuscan gold and painted our bathroom a deep emerald green, which inspired stencils of bat rays and turtles. We barbecued oysters and ate them on the deck, tossing the shells into the flower beds below. On Sundays we sprawled in the sunroom, reading the paper and drinking French roast till noon. In short, a comforting dailiness was returning to our lives; in the car, at the table, in the bedroom, Alex's face was becoming, simply, Alex.

If only Nicole Wolf's name didn't keep popping up. She was Alex's physical therapist. Born and raised in London, she'd migrated here for her graduate work, first at Boston University, then the University of Southern California. I didn't doubt the extent of Nicole's knowledge or how important she had been in Alex's recovery. The limp was gone, and Alex had stopped taking pain meds; both her legs were stronger, the calf muscles taut and well defined. She was in the best shape of her life, Alex told me; she felt "fantastic."

I had no idea how much money Alex had spent on Nicole, nor did I want to know. I just wondered why, at this point, Nicole was still needed. I also wondered why she was beginning to prescribe our menus, as well as our personal care products.

The first time I'd seen Nicole was at the gym. Indulging my curiosity about her, I had stopped there one day after work. Alex had told me that Nicole was "a nice-looking woman with short brown hair." I was not prepared for the bronze super-human I saw on the treadmill, resplendent in a vermilion bra top and black shorts. Her arms and thighs were gorgeously muscled, and you could have broken a plate on her stomach. Her dark hair fit snugly around her head, reminding me of armor. As I approached, Alex, who was on the neighboring treadmill, saw me and waved, then said something to Nicole, who turned her head my way and smiled. Her teeth were alarmingly white, the incisors curved and larger than normal, ready for anything.

Not long after that she came for dinner, her first time here (as far as I knew). Once again I was struck by her radiant health—teeth, nails, skin, hair, all sleek and shining, as if they were living their own robust lives and Nicole was their host. She was wearing an indigo suit, a white blouse, and a pair of gold earrings that I realized were vaulting gymnasts. When she shook my hand, she hurt me a little.

Naturally I was uneasy about this formidable figure who spent hours and hours exercising half-naked with my partner, manipulating her limbs, instructing her to do God knew what. I studied them surreptitiously, behind the irises Nicole had brought (I have to give her credit: She brought flowers and wine, she didn't talk too much, and she left before I started wishing she would). I never saw any sign of flirtation between her and Alex. In fact, Nicole focused her avidity on me, asking me all about my business and how I liked being an entrepreneur and did I know a good accountant. Alex, listening to us, was gracious and at ease, happy to see that her roasted eggplant pizza was such a success. Across the table, in a new, peach-colored blouse, with her dark-honey hair swept up, she was breathtaking. If anyone was enamored that night, it was me.

~

Dana finished her cosmopolitan and ordered another. The server looked over at me. "Another merlot?"

"Sure."

It had been a bad day. The memory function on our fax machine had failed, and several orders were floating in the ethers; Ricky called in with a broken shoulder (skateboarding); and Garret had managed to back the new van into a light pole, mangling the fender. When Dana suggested a drink after work, I jumped on it. We were sitting in the lounge at Skates on the Bay, which fortunately wasn't crowded. Only three other tables were occupied, and these with quiet couples.

Dana squeezed a lime wedge into her frosty pink drink and shrugged. "At least it wasn't another car he backed into. He said he'd pay the deductible."

"That's okay," I said. "No need." I was feeling expansive, restored, thanks to the wine. We were sitting at a table beside a massive salt-stained window. A few feet away, two seagulls rocked on the gray waves. "How long did they say the repair will take?"

"They said it'll be ready on Friday. How long will Ricky be out?"

"I don't know. Maybe two weeks—he's not sure; he needs medical clearance."

Dana gave a sigh. "*Two weeks.*" She shifted in her chair, looked at me dubiously. "Maybe Alex can come in?"

I shook my head. It had been more than a month since Alex had helped us out. "She doesn't have the time. She and Nicole are starting a business."

"Doing what?"

"Well, I'm not sure how they'll market it, but it's a two-pronged approach to self-improvement—not to be confused with spiritual growth, of course. Nicole will deal with the body, and Alex will be a sort of beauty therapist."

"A beauty *therapist?*"

I nodded. "She's taking some kind of accelerated program, learning all about the latest cosmetic techniques—lasers, resurfacing, chemicals peels, fillers, Botox. She wants to evaluate people and tell them what their options are. She's researching clinics so she can do referrals."

"Ambitious," Dana murmured.

"Oh, yeah. It's all she's talking about lately. That and our diet. She's purged the fridge. I don't think there's anything in there right now but kale and soy milk."

Dana looked puzzled. "You two have always eaten healthy stuff; I didn't think there was anything to improve on."

"Well, Alex does. And she hasn't stopped at the kitchen; she's gone through the bathroom, too, tossed out the L'Oreal and Jergens. She's got us using this pricey line of skin-care products from England. Splendor, it's called. Nicole turned her on to it."

The fog had rolled back in; surprisingly close, a sailboat slowly came into being. I took another swallow of wine. "Nicole Wolf," I sneered. "I bet that isn't even her name. I bet her real name is

Hortense. Hortense Broadbottom."

Dana laughed.

"And everyone made fun of her because she was fat and pasty, so she turned herself into a hard-body and sprayed on a tan." Frowning, I ran a finger along the slick edge of my glass. "And then she came to America and started stalking my girlfriend."

"Are you *jealous?*" Dana said.

"I'm getting there. All the time she spends with Alex. And that accent she pours on that makes everything she says sound so god-damn charming." I took the red plastic toothpick from Dana's napkin and snapped it in half.

"Things were going so good"—I arched an eyebrow at Dana—"yes, especially that, and then Alex climbed on this health-and-beauty kick. She gets out of bed at night and makes notes. Every five seconds she has a new idea for the business. Naturally she's spending a lot more time with Hortense."

Dana folded her arms on the table and looked at me squarely. "Shelley, you have nothing to worry about. Alex adores you. Besides, she'd never cheat; it's just not who she is—you know that."

I did. No one who knew Alex would question her honor. Her license plate cover read: DO THE RIGHT THING—EVEN WHEN NO ONE IS LOOKING. She once told me that she could understand the impulse to cheat; she just couldn't fathom anyone actually doing it.

"It's not so strange," Dana went on, "that Alex is starting this business. She lived it; she's a walking advertisement." I turned my head and looked at the bar, regarded the colorful rows of liquor endlessly reflected in the mirror behind them. Bars made me think of Christmas.

"There are worse things she could be into," Dana said. "What if she suddenly wanted to do one of those extreme sports—skiing off cliffs. Ice climbing. What if she wanted to move to LA and become a *soap star?*"

~

*Looks for Life.* Alex was the one who came up with the name, as well as the investors. Given her business savvy and connections, money would not be a major problem. Lucky girl, that Nicole, who I knew was saddled with student loans and presumably a sizable car payment (she had recently acquired a black Mercedes SUV).

As a way of marketing Looks for Life, Alex had begun writing a book about her ordeal. The first part, she told me, would recount the accident and consequent surgeries; the second part would explain the procedures on her face; the last part of the book would "demystify" cosmetic surgery and help people understand their many options. "I know that my case is exceptional," Alex said, "but that's just the point, letting people know that amazing things are possible, that they don't have to live with looks they don't like."

Although I had never confessed this to anyone, it frightened me a little that Alex had molted her prior visage with such apparent ease. If it cost her anything beyond money, she had not let on.

"But is that always the answer?" I said. "What about liking yourself just as you are? I mean, people born disfigured or scarred in accidents, I can see the value of surgery then, but not for—"

"Not for the rest of humanity? So if you are merely ugly you should learn to live with it?"

She was looking at me in a way I didn't recognize. I was used to returning to her eyes for reassurance; velvet brown, flecked with gold, they were the same eyes I had fallen into the day we met—now they made my stomach clench.

"Sounds like that old myth," she went on, "about adversity conferring character. Why should people suffer? I don't think there's anything wrong with wanting to make life easier."

"It just seems like the wrong message," I said, faltering.

"But hair dye and makeup are okay? That's absurd. You can shave your legs, but you have to keep the cellulite. You can cover up your broken veins with makeup but not lasers." She reached up and removed her earrings, dropped them on the granite countertop; she looked bored. "Shelley, surgeons can fix more these days than cleft palates and cataracts."

I felt confused. Who was this woman with all the answers? Where was the Alex who had sidled away from arguments, leaving me to reach my own conclusions?

"I know," I said, "but people in general are not beautiful. You would have them all running to plastic surgeons? How many people can afford that?"

She regarded me with exaggerated patience. In a flat voice she said, "You're right. Most people can't afford it. But then I won't be dealing with 'most people.' Obviously."

And there it was again, that snobbery. Where had that come from? Alex had never condescended; it was one of the things people loved about her—the way she accepted their foibles, urged them to laugh at themselves and have fun with life.

Our friends had noticed it, too, this change. Maureen and Lorrie, the couple we were closest to, the women we had spent ten days in Hawaii with, mentioned to me that Alex was "more removed" now, that they sometimes felt uncertain around her, and not because of her beauty. It was something else, they said; they weren't sure what. "She's so ... " Maureen paused. "So eloquent." Which was not a word that customarily sprang to mind when you thought of Alex.

We weren't spending a lot of time with Maureen and Lorrie, or any of our other friends, these days. With everything she had going on, Alex had little time for socializing, though she had mentioned making some new friends at the gym—people with similar goals, I imagined. People with perfect bodies.

And yes, I was becoming self-conscious about mine. I am a middle-aged woman, reasonably attractive, only a few extra pounds—less than ten, I'm sure. I have short, ash-blonde hair (more ash than blonde now), which I don't and won't color, and, aside from mascara and moisturizer, I put nothing on my face. Aging, I have learned, is a matter of forgiving: Pardon each new wrinkle and spot as it arises, and you're done with it. I was beginning to lose that assurance, beginning to pause at the mirror and wonder what Alex saw when she looked at me, what treatments she might recommend. And what about my body? What about the way her hands had paused last week on my waist, on the twin bulges over my belt, the way she looked at me and said nothing? What was she thinking then?

~

Dana drummed her fingers on the steering wheel. We were in the van, stuck in traffic on Highway 80. In the back was our last delivery, six flats of cilantro for Dillard's Nursery in Emeryville. Ricky was making deliveries in Lafayette, though he was probably done by now.

"Hope we get there before they close," said Dana.

I tried to see what was going on in front of us, but there was only a river of cars and trucks. "Maybe there's an accident."

"I doubt it. Highway 80 is always bad now." She put on the left turn signal, then turned it off. "Left lane's no better than this one. Tell me a story."

The sun was beginning to set over the bay, and the windows of the high-rise condominiums on the left were blazing gold. Summer was nearly over; this morning, when I left the house, I got my first heartbreaking whiff of autumn, a mixture of leaves and smoke, a stirring sharpness. Beautiful, serious autumn.

I couldn't smell autumn at the moment, only the exhaust of a few thousand vehicles. On the right, a big burgundy pickup surged ahead. There was a decal on the cab window of four flying ducks, and below that the words: IF IT FLIES IT DIES. "Morons," I murmured, settling back into the seat. "I feel fat," I said.

Dana kept her eyes on the road. "You are in no way fat."

"Old, then."

"You're not that either." She looked over. "What's up?"

"I don't know. I just wonder if maybe I should put more effort into myself."

"What do you mean?"

"Oh, you know—hair, skin, teeth. Maybe I'll get my teeth whitened."

Dana accelerated a few feet. "Is this about Nicole again? Because her teeth do not look natural. Nothing about Nicole looks very natural." Nicole had stopped by the nursery a couple weeks before; Dana had given her a tour.

"But that body," I said, gazing now at the side of a red Jeep that had what looked like bullet holes in the door.

"So she's got a nice body." She looked over at me again, tapped my thigh. "Got news for you, dearie. You are way prettier than Nicole."

I smiled back. "Thanks." What would I do without Dana? We had known each other longer than I had been with Alex. Dana was a rare breed: a woman who had left the lesbian circuit when she fell for *a man*—a geologist named Bodie. I didn't hold it against her; I liked Bodie, a big bear of a man who made me laugh.

"And like I said, I don't think Nicole's after your woman." The traffic began to break up; we were gaining ground. "Remember when she came to your place for dinner and asked all those questions about our business? Well, she was the same way when I showed her the nursery. She's focused on one thing, and Alex is the way she can get it. I don't think she's a home wrecker; I think she's a gold digger."

It was true that Nicole was the one who had approached Alex about starting a business. It was also true that Nicole had accumulated some debt.

"How's it going?" Dana said. "The business."

"It's going. They've found some office space near the gym, and Alex is working with an editor; they're doing the final revisions on the book."

"That was fast. So she has a publisher?"

"Oh, yeah. That wasn't any trouble at all. Horrible accident, miraculous surgery—throw in Malik's name and a few before-and-after pictures, and you have a bestseller."

"You think?"

"Absolutely. Alex has already told me that she'll be doing book tours soon. I wouldn't be surprised if she wound up on TV. Oprah's network."

"You're probably right," Dana said, nodding.

"And I bet Hortense figured all that out from day one."

One thing for sure: I could probably afford to spend a little more time primping (I showered, dressed, and was out the door in under twenty minutes), but no way was I going to wind up like the woman in the Lexus who had just edged by us. For a moment our eyes met, and she tried to smile—perhaps she thought she managed it; what I saw was a grimace, the skin so taut it appeared to be covered with cellophane. Her eyelids were drooping under the weight of false lashes, her mouth was a fire-red gash, and her hair—the color of cantaloupes—was elaborately rigged on top of her head. She was fierce, this woman. She had time in a stranglehold, and she was not giving up an inch. She was losing, and she knew it, but she was not giving up.

~

It was a scene from a Lifetime movie. Candles burned low; a pair of cold halibut filets in the pan, their lemon-butter sauce turned to wax; and me, slouched at the table, finishing the bottle of dinner wine.

"You're still up?" Alex said when she walked in. It was 11:42. I edged a hard look her way and nodded toward the stove. She glanced at the fish and frowned.

"You should have eaten. We ran late. There's so much to do, all the paperwork to get ready. You know how it was, starting the nursery." No apology, I noticed.

"Alex, you've been with Nicole four nights this week. Can't you find some time during the day? After your workout?"

She hung her jacket on the hook near the door and headed for the study. "Malik warned me about this."

"About what?" I followed her down the hall.

"About jealousy. That you might become unreasonably jealous."

This irked me, the thought of her and Malik discussing my feelings as if they were possible side effects.

She sat down at her desk and raised the cover of her laptop. "I just need to check my e-mail."

"I don't think I'm being unreasonable," I said.

She kept her eyes on the computer screen. "Maybe not. But I want you to understand that I just can't give you all the time you need right now. I'm starting a business; I'm writing a book. I need to stay focused."

I stood there staring at her faultless profile.

"I love you." She sighed, looking up. "I never stopped. What do I need to do to prove it?"

"Act like it."

Perhaps because of the wine and my fatigue, the words came out with less authority than I'd intended, more a plea than a command. Clearly it was time to go to bed. I turned to leave, and Alex said, softly, "I can do that."

I stopped, surprised. "I can do that," she repeated, rising from the chair. She smiled at me, a smile so true, so unexpected, that I felt it in the soles of my feet. She opened her arms, approached me; for a long moment she simply held me close. "I love you," she breathed into my neck, and then her mouth was on mine and she was kissing me like it was her dying wish, and somewhere between there and the sofa we fell upon, I was convinced.

~

It was two days later that I saw the notes from Nicole. I was in the kitchen washing up some breakfast dishes; Alex was in the shower. She had left her phone on the table, and I heard it chime, indicating a message. I knew she was waiting for a call from her publisher, so I dried my hands, picked up the phone, and saw that it was a text. I wasn't in the habit of reading Alex's messages, and I'm not sure what made me do it then, but I opened the text and saw these words, right under Nicole's name: CAN'T W8T 2 DO U. C U AT 8. This was followed by a winking emoticon.

My chest was concrete; I couldn't breathe. I read the message again, and again. *Do u.* Maybe she was talking about a new exercise. Maybe it was gym-speak, slang for workout. I hit the phone's BACK key and found two earlier messages from Nicole that hadn't been deleted, one from yesterday: I LOVE YOUR LIPS, though it could have been, I WANT YOUR MOUTH. Nicole had deployed two symbols, a heart for the verb and a pair of lips for the object. Quite an arsenal she must have had in that phone. The other message was even more ominous, just three little words: I LOVED IT.

Now I knew why Nicole had been so pleasant to me the night she came to dinner. She was winning. She had won.

~

Alex's remorse was not overwhelming. "I'm sorry," she said in a voice that didn't break. No tears. No abashed looks at the floor. "I was waiting. I wanted to be sure." I think she was annoyed at me for intruding on her privacy. I had brought it on myself, she seemed to imply, her back to the kitchen counter, her arms tightly folded.

Within a week she was moved out, and our paths didn't cross after that. Although her office was just a few miles away, I didn't see Alex again until I went into Barnes & Noble nearly a year later and found her book—sure enough—on the bestseller table. *A Surgeon's Gift*, it was called. On the cover was a misty photo with a pastel-blue background: a pair of hands gently holding a scalpel. Good lord, I thought.

On the back cover was a blurb about Malik, with his photo alongside. Dark eyes, ravishing white smile. The Soul Snatcher, Dana called him. Beneath Malik's picture was a larger one of Alex. She was looking at the camera straight on, much as she had looked at me that last time. I gave a gasp, which the people near me must have heard. Over the past few months, my memories had defaulted to Alex before the accident, when she wore hats and danced in her store and laughed like nobody else. Here was the woman Alex had become. Lovely as she was, I'd forgotten all about her.

# Remediation

I kid you not. This thing looked like it had been in a furnace."

Joyce unscrews the top of her orange thermos. Sunlight flashes across the rings on her swollen fingers as she pours herself more Baileys Irish Cream.

"She wanted to know what it needed. I told her it needed water. She said, 'But it looks sick. Isn't there something I can spray on it?' 'Yes,' I said, 'water.'"

Joyce leans back in the deck chair and laughs. Her hair—a sweeping gold crest—doesn't move.

I've had three gin and tonics myself, and I'm feeling great. I love to make Joyce laugh. "Most of them come in too late," I add. "They come in carrying these corpses and want to know how to fix them."

Joyce peels the cellophane strip off a fresh pack of Virginia Slims and shakes her head. "Well, I can't talk. I have to buy fake plants."

"Which is perfectly fine!" I say, throwing up my hands. "I wish more of our customers would buy vinyl. Believe me, it's not easy selling plants to some of these people. Yesterday one of our regulars—the Grave Digger, we call him—bought a gorgeous red dahlia. I could hear it screaming as he carried it out."

This brings on another bout of Joyce's wheezing laughter, which ends with a mild coughing attack. "Stop it, Molly," she says, wiping her eyes with the back of her hand. "Right now. You're killing me."

Doug comes out on the deck then, shoots us a look on his way to the grill. In one hand he has a plate of raw chicken, in the other a pair of tongs.

Doug doesn't like Joyce. Maybe because she makes a lot more money than he does. Maybe because she has a federal job with a pension and paid holidays. Maybe because she paid for my abortion when I was twenty-two, with two babies, and Doug was out of work, and the last thing I wanted in this world was another child. Maybe he dislikes Joyce simply because she is no longer beautiful.

"I'm going to go set the table," I tell her, getting to my feet. "You stay put. Relax."

"You're a doll," she says, beaming up at me. At fifty-three, she still has striking cheekbones, especially when she smiles, which is often. Good skin, too. Of course, she works at it, buys expensive moisturizers and makeup. Her blue eyes she accentuates with a lavish amount of mascara and liner. Her nose is small and slightly crooked, with a crease at the bridge. Her mouth is nicely shaped, and her teeth are tidy: You'd never know that most of them were ruined in a God-awful accident many years ago, when her head plowed through the windshield of her red Camaro.

Doug comes back inside as I am putting silverware on the table. "We're going to eat in half an hour," he says. "You two going to be ready?"

"Sure."

"Where did you take her today?"

"Napa Valley. We went wine-tasting."

"Bet she loved that."

Ignoring the smirk on his face, I buff a knife blade with my shirttail and set it back down. "It was fun. We went on the tram at Sterling, had lunch at the Rutherford Grill. I had salmon, and she had ribs."

Doug snorts. "The last thing she needs is a plate of ribs."

"Would you just can it, please?" Irritated, I brush past him, and he follows me into the kitchen.

"Well, look at her. She's probably gained twenty pounds since she was here last. And the smoking—that's just idiotic. I thought you said she quit."

Doug is a fitness freak. His waist is only an inch bigger than it was thirty years ago. One room in our house is filled with gym equipment, sleek chrome beasts that he mounts in sickness or in health every day of his life. Had I known this thirty years ago, I might not have married him. Honestly. You'd never guess how amusing Doug could be in the old bacon-and-egg days, before that regiment of machines came in and commandeered the guest room.

I stay thin no matter what I eat or do (something that infuriates my daughter); I just have one of those metabolisms. Still, Doug chides me for not exercising. I need cardio workouts, he claims, weight training. My daily walks are not enough to combat the effects of aging. That's the word he uses: *combat*.

Joyce, with her Baileys and Virginia Slims, he considers a bad influence, though there's more to it than that. He thinks she looks down on him for not making more money. Doug manages a tile and stone company not far from the nursery where I'm employed. How we arrived at these places isn't clear, but things have worked out okay. We have, for example, the best-looking yard in the subdivision.

While it's true that Joyce makes fun of Doug, it has nothing to do with his income or career. She just thinks Doug should lighten up. Last night, when he marched through the living room intoning the time, Joyce gave me a look of mock fear and started to giggle. "Doesn't he remind you of the Terminator?" she whispered.

I nodded. "He does have a way of ending things. Like fun." And when he heard our peals of laughter on his way up the stairs, I knew how pissed off he must have been. You can imagine the cold shoulder I got when I finally went to bed.

Despite our big lunch, Joyce and I have no trouble polishing off the grilled tandoori chicken legs, steamed corn cobs, and wilted spinach Doug has prepared. He is an impressive cook and takes pride in his efforts; you just need to remember to compliment him. We do, several times over, and he expands with delight.

"What wineries did you go to today?" he says amiably.

Joyce looks at me. "Beringer, right? And the one with the tram—Sterling. And the other one—it had a funny name."

"Peju."

"That was my favorite," she says. "The stained glass."

"Did you buy any wine?" Doug asks.

Joyce nods. "Two bottles."

"What were they?"

She shrugs, lifts the ear of corn from her plate. "I don't know. I just liked them."

A few years ago Doug took a wine class and learned just enough to make him borderline obnoxious. I head off any further questions on the subject by asking Joyce how her work is going. She actually has an interesting job, not something you'd find on a bulletin board or in a career counseling office. Joyce tours decommissioned military bases and helps decide what to do with them. Some are sold to the public and become private airports or manufacturing plants or housing developments; others harbor so much potential contamination that they are deemed "Superfund sites" and are slated for massive cleanups; most hang somewhere in between, not dangerous enough to spend money on, not safe enough to sell. These are the ones that languish for decades behind razor-topped fences, home to spiny lizards and burrowing spiders and the occasional exhausted flock of geese. After assessment, the sale-worthy bases are listed with local reuse authorities, with whom Joyce negotiates fair market value. She seems to like what she does and never complains about the travel involved, at least not to me. In fact, I think she gets a kick out of it, even after all these years, judging from the paraphernalia she sends me from various towns: shot glasses, key rings, refrigerator magnets, coffee mugs. Some of it I throw away; the rest of it gets shoved in the back of the linen closet. I pull out a few things when she visits, but she never comments on them.

"Oh, they're keeping me busy," Joyce says. "Sales are slow because of the ERs—we're a decade out on some of them—but bases are closing faster than we can evaluate them." She shakes her head. "All the cutbacks."

By now I know what most of Joyce's acronyms stand for: ER is Environmental Remediation, which can mean anything from removing leaking solvents to stripping away asbestos, mop-ups the government can't afford.

"What are they going to do about that old Mothball Fleet?" Doug says.

"They still use a lot of those ships."

"For what?"

Joyce puts down her corn. "Well," she says, counting off on glistening fingers, "training marines, firefighters, rescue workers, oil spill response teams—"

"What about the pollution?" Doug interrupts. "All that corrosion and paint chipping into the bay." I give him the eye, but he won't look my way.

"Some of the ships are scrapped, but most of them are maintained.

And ready," she adds pointedly. "They inspect that fleet every day, you know."

Doug ignores this and reaches for more chicken. I know he gets on her nerves, that she tolerates him mainly for my sake.

"Connor spoke with Al Gore last week," I say to Doug. This is an act of self-sacrifice, bringing up Joyce's son. Connor is a lieutenant colonel in the Marines, and ever since he was born I've been hearing about his triumphs: walking at eight months, talking at twelve months, Eagle Scout, high school quarterback. Back at their home in Ann Arbor, Connor's bedroom remains precisely the way he left it, shipshape quarters bedecked with trophies and pennants.

"No kidding," Doug says without inflection.

Joyce eagerly launches into a more vivid description of the awards dinner she told me about yesterday: the eight Marines who were honored, the floral arrangements, the fancy food, the arrival of the former Vice President. I know that Doug is probably wondering what this gala cost the taxpayers, while I'm thinking about how tense things are in Afghanistan and how glad I am that my son is not a soldier—to hell with the badges and ribbons.

Winding down, Joyce wipes her hands on her napkin and asks how Adam is doing.

"Great," I say. "Still at the bike shop. He's gotten into holistic medicine—did I tell you that? This summer he took a course in crystal therapy."

Doug glowers at me from across the table, and I see he's not thrilled that I just shared this piece of news.

"Well, good for him," Joyce says. "I think there's a lot behind that holistic medicine. I've read about some of it. What about Amanda? How are things in Boulder?"

At the mention of Amanda's name, my diaphragm does a quick squeeze. Joyce is wearing her poker face.

Amanda lives in Boulder, where she waits tables at a trendy tapas restaurant and dates a married man whose name I do not know because she won't trust me with it. I told Joyce about this affair when Amanda told me—nearly two years ago. Doug, thank God, doesn't have a clue.

I shrug. "Good, I guess. You know Amanda—not a lot of dialogue. She did say that she enrolled at the university again." She'd dropped out the first time. "She wants to study evolutionary biology. I don't know what she plans to do with it."

"Sounds brainy," says Joyce. "Amanda's bright, no question about that."

Joyce has always been fond of Amanda—even took her in during the summer she was fourteen and so full of hormones and rebellion that I was reduced to cowering in her presence. "Send her here," Joyce urged and, sobbing into the phone, I agreed. Amanda was only too happy to get away from Doug and me, probably thought she'd have free rein all summer, and perhaps she did. I don't know what happened in those three months, but when Amanda came home, she was someone I could live with, a girl who looked at me when we spoke and even, on occasion, smiled.

"When is Katy due?" I ask.

"In January. Better winter than summer—well, except for the icy sidewalks. It was ninety-seven the day Tucker was born."

Both Joyce and I have a son and a daughter, though hers are a few years older and more accomplished than mine. Katy, who is a CPA, is as sensible as Connor is disciplined. This galls me, I admit, considering how permissive Joyce has always been. I try not to be resentful, to compare—Joyce adores my kids and unfailingly praises their modest achievements. Still, I wish I had better news to give her. I would at least like to tell her that Amanda has come to her senses and is no longer dating a married man. Can you even call that dating?

I don't think so. I think you have to use a different verb.

Doug pushes back his chair and asks if anyone wants coffee. "No, thanks," says Joyce. "I think I will pop outside for a smoke, though. Delicious meal, Doug."

I clear the rest of the table while he starts loading the dishwasher. Through the kitchen window I watch Joyce blow a long stream of smoke into the summer evening. Her head is resting against the back of the chair; her ankles are crossed. Behind her the mandevilla vine bursts with white flowers.

I turn to Doug, who is rinsing the chicken platter. In his large, soapy hands the plate looks small.

"Well, you were pretty goddamned rude."

He looks at me as if he had no idea this was coming. "What?"

"That crack about the Mothball Fleet, for one thing. You know how she feels about that."

He frowns, turns back to the sink. "I hate it when she starts her flag-waving."

"*Flag-waving?* She was talking about her job, and I was the one who brought it up."

"And that long windy spiel about Connor and Al Gore. Jesus, I thought she'd never shut up about that." He shoves the platter into the dishwasher. "Why did you have to tell her about Adam and the crystal therapy?"

"Because I'm not ashamed of it," I hiss. *I am ashamed of you*, I want to add, but I stop myself: Things are bad enough right now, and Joyce won't be leaving till Monday.

~

"This was her favorite song." Joyce says. "She wrote it after she and George Jones split up. That woman sure had some bad luck. You know she had twenty-six major surgeries?"

We are talking about Tammy Wynette, and "Till I Can Make It On My Own" is the song we are listening to. It is playing on Joyce's portable CD player, which she brings on all her travels, along with that orange thermos.

I would never think to do something like that, travel with a CD player. It's one of the things I admire about Joyce, the ways she entertains herself. I would also never think to buy country music, though I find myself enjoying these songs, especially the toe-tapping ones like "Your Good Girl's Gonna Go Bad."

"What did she die of?"

"Blood clot. She died in her sleep." Joyce sighs. "Boy, that's the way to go, isn't it? I guess she earned that, after all she went through."

Joyce, by the way, has gone through a few things herself.

When she was nineteen, her parents and younger sister were killed in a bus accident on their way to the Grand Canyon. Not long after that, Joyce drove her Camaro into a highway median and spent the next year and a half in and out of surgery.

When she was twenty-two, she married a cop with a drinking problem. One day, he accidentally set fire to their living room; the next day, he drove through their fence. Joyce forgave him the fire and the fence, but the night he made the mistake of raising a fist to her she felled him with a frozen pork roast and tied him up before he came to. Which is even more impressive when you consider that she was seven months pregnant at the time.

Her second husband was a good man with a bad heart. Three years into the marriage, he bought them a brand-new lakefront home, leaving her with the staggering mortgage when he died soon after on a morning jog.

Both husbands were good for something, Joyce says: Connor and Katy. But the true love of her life—and she readily admits this—is my brother Rick, whom she dated in high school. A sweet-talking recreant with gorgeous blue eyes, Rick has about a two-minute attention span, and poor Joyce, pretty as she was, never stood a chance of keeping him. The most I can say about my brother is that he had the sense to stay single. Despite the pain he caused her, despite his thoughtless ways, Joyce has never uttered a word against Rick and in fact still sends him cards and birthday gifts. Doug says it's pathetic the way Joyce "hangs on to that jerk." I think she has no choice. I think that's just the way Joyce loves people, full-on and nonstop, whether they're worth it or not.

Joyce picks up her thermos, pours the last dregs.

"The sugar in that doesn't keep you up?" I ask.

She chuckles. "Not that I've noticed." It's true that the only sound I've heard from the guest room is some pretty serious snoring.

"You turn the big five-o this March, don't you?" she asks.

"I'm afraid so."

Her crow's feet deepen as she gives me a broad smile. Joyce has the best smile; it goes right up into her eyes. "Well, Molly girl, I'm coming out for that one. We have to celebrate."

Alarm flutters through me. Typically Joyce visits every couple years. March is only six months away.

"Really?"

She nods firmly. "Absolutely. Fifty is the big one, the reality check. You need to be prepared. You need to pamper yourself. Four-star hotel, room service, massage. That's for starters." She pauses. "Unless you have other plans."

"*I* don't. I'm not sure what Doug has in mind, though."

"Well, we can always do something the day after. Extend the party. Maybe you can come to Ann Arbor," she says, raising her eyebrows hopefully.

"I don't know. It's hard for me to get time off in the spring."

"Oh, that's right," Joyce says. "Planting season."

I probably should have been more gracious. It's sweet of her to want to celebrate my birthday. Three years ago, when Joyce turned fifty, it didn't occur to me to make a big deal of it. I think I sent her a card and a gift certificate. I'm not good about answering her letters either.

I study her now, her grand golden hair—how *does* she maintain that?—her stylish white jacket, strained across her ample waist; her short legs in fuchsia capris; her feet wedged into tiny sandals, and I think how true to herself she is, how *fearless*. All her life she has been this way. I remember sledding with her, how she always went for the steepest hills, her arms outstretched, her hair streaming behind her. I remember how she laughed as she flew across Echo Pond, the ice cracking beneath her skates. I remember the long summers we shared, the things she talked me into—like the day we bought new bathing suits at Thurman's department store. We were walking back to the bus stop when suddenly she steered me through the thick glass doors of the Sheraton hotel, straight through the lobby and out to the pool, where we swam and lounged with the paying guests. I've never known anyone like Joyce. It must be a rare gene, this knack for turning life into play.

"You're amazing," I tell her, voicing my thoughts.

She looks at me, surprised. "Well, thanks. You're not so bad yourself."

"How do you do it?" I ask. "Seriously. All that enthusiasm. How do you stay so up?"

She shrugs. "Just lucky, I guess. I don't worry about things, never have." She laughs. "Could be I'm just a fool."

"You are no fool," I assure her.

~

113

I wake the next morning with a rhythmic headache and imagine a white ram kicking the back of my skull.

What did I expect? White wine with lunch; gin and tonics on the deck; then, at dinner, a hefty glass of merlot I was almost smart enough to say no to. I turn onto my back, wincing a little, and look over at Doug, who is standing broad-shouldered in front of the dresser mirror, running a comb though his graying blond hair. In a red polo shirt and khaki pants, he exudes irreproachable health. The poster boy for Centrum Silver.

"Hey," he says.

"Hey."

He walks over and sits on the edge of the bed, runs a hand up my leg. "Just one more day, then I have you all to myself." He gives me a kiss on the cheek. The fresh minty smell of his breath makes me nauseous, and I turn my face away.

"Where are you taking her today?" he asks.

"San Francisco." The itinerary appalls me: BART train to the city, lunch twenty floors above the ground, cable car to Union Square, a million other shoppers. I can barely manage the prospect of a shower.

Doug gives an exaggerated sigh. "Haven't you two done all that? Alcatraz, the Golden Gate, Fisherman's Wharf. How many times does she have to haul you over there?"

"She wants to have brunch at the Mark Hopkins, and then she wants to go to Macy's. Connor's birthday's coming up—she's on a quest."

"Sounds like a lot of money." He gets up and walks back to the dresser, pulls on his watch.

"Speaking of money, do we have bonds?"

He looks over, frowns. "What do you mean?"

"Are we invested in municipal bonds?"

"Yeah, I guess. We're diversified."

"Joyce says that most people don't have enough in bonds."

Doug shakes his head. "So now she's an investment expert?" Joyce does dish out the advice, I'll give him that.

I rise up on one elbow. "You know what she did yesterday? There's this metal pig sculpture in front of the Rutherford Grill. She stuck a cigarette in its mouth."

"Why?"

"I don't know. She'd had some wine; she thought it was funny. She couldn't stop laughing. People were looking at her and looking away." I glance down at Doug's new Nikes and remember something else to offer him. "And she told our waiter he had bedroom eyes."

Doug groans. "Oh, God. She's still doing that flirty stuff? That worked about forty years ago." Both Doug and I grew up in Ann Arbor, and he's known Joyce as long as I have. Sometimes I wonder if he once had a thing for her, back in the day, if maybe he asked her out at some point and she said no. Which would explain a lot.

~

Joyce pulls a limp green bean from her Bloody Mary and begins chewing it. Her eyes dart about the room, taking in everything: the gleaming mahogany bar, the huge vase of sunflowers, the waiters in their white shirts and black ties. Beneath a layer of makeup her cheeks are flushed; she is smiling, almost constantly, so thrilled she is to be here. The Top of the Mark! Far below us, hunched in the wind-whipped bay, is the island of Alcatraz, a gray rock topped with long, low buildings and a handful of salt-scoured trees.

Joyce has just related a story she has told me before: the time my mother was pulled over by a state trooper when she was on her way to Florida. Five years ago Joyce helped my mother move down there, another kindness Joyce shrugs off ("I didn't have anything else going on that week, and a road trip sounded like fun"). The facts of the story didn't change in the retelling: There they were, cruising along in the passing lane, breaking the law, radio blaring, mouths going, while a cop—flashers on and sirens wailing—chased them for two miles. "Good gosh, was he mad!" Joyce said. "And you know your mother, how scared she is of authority figures." (No, I did not know this. How is it I didn't know?)

Thanks to the scrambled eggs and Bloody Mary, I'm feeling almost normal. If Joyce was hungover this morning, she didn't show it. I've never known her to meet a new day with anything but readiness, and this is not the first time I've envied her formidable constitution.

"What a great meal," she says. "I was famished."

I don't say what I'm thinking, that the meal wasn't great at all: The eggs were cold and runny, and the sausage was rubbery. Which is what you can expect from tourist traps like this, though Joyce always insists on them.

Unable to stand it any longer, I let Joyce know that she has a bit of food on her face. She licks a finger, rubs it vigorously against her cheek. "Did I get it?"

"You're good," I tell her. I don't mention the fact that her mascara is smudged under one eye; that's something she can find on her own. Doug's right—she uses way too much eye makeup. Perfume, too.

"I'm glad it's not foggy," I say, nodding toward the bay.

"It's lovely." Joyce nods. "Such blue, blue water. And all the sailboats. I can see why you left Michigan." She lays her puffy ringed fingers on my forearm. "I miss you like the dickens, though."

"It's hard," I say, avoiding an outright lie.

"Too bad Doug couldn't join us," she says, being nice. "Does he have to work every Sunday?"

"Yeah. People do their projects on the weekends."

Joyce sighs, rests her chin in her palm. "You know, I kid you a lot about Doug and how straitlaced he is, but honey, you could have done a lot worse. I mean, how many men cook and do the dishes *willingly?*"

I roll my eyes. "You think he came that way?"

Joyce laughs. "Well, he adores you, I know that." She regards me tenderly and says, "I like knowing that you're in good hands."

I squirm at this and look around for our waiter. "Another Bloody?"

"Definitely." She leans over, cups her hand around her mouth. "We can check out our waiter's cute butt again!"

~

A few weeks later, two days before Thanksgiving, I come home to a somber message from Katy on the answering machine. She says she will call again in the evening, that she needs to talk to me. "It's important," she adds, her voice breaking, and my heart beats faster. She doesn't answer when I call back, so I leave a message of my own and then call Joyce, who is also unavailable. Her voice recording is clear and friendly, encouraging me to leave as long a message as I'd like, and for a moment I forget that she is not on the line. Startled by the beep, I stumble for words and finally manage to say that Katy has phoned me and I'm worried. "Call me, okay?"

I can't imagine why Katy, who is as independent as her mother, would be calling me; I like her well enough, but we're not especially close. Could she be in some sort of trouble? Maybe I shouldn't have called Joyce.

Before dinner I try phoning Katy again, but there is still no answer. I sit down at the table, pick up my fork, put it down.

"Maybe there was a fire," I say, my eyes widening as I consider the likelihood of this. The orange thermos. Joyce fast asleep. A cigarette smoldering on the carpet.

Doug, who is steadily consuming his tuna salad, looks up from his plate. "I doubt it's anything that dramatic."

"Well, you'd think Joyce would have called by now. Maybe she was in an accident." I picture her in a hospital bed, pierced with tubes. Or maybe she has some awful illness. Maybe Katy called to tell me her mother has cancer … all those toxic sites she inspected, radiation leaking from God knows where.

Doug takes a long pull on his spring water and sets down the bottle. "She's probably in one of her *meetings*," he says, saturating the last word with sarcasm.

"Not at this hour. It's nine o'clock in Michigan."

He shrugs. "You don't know where she is."

Which is true. The world is full of ghost barracks and naval boneyards. Joyce could be anywhere.

"You need to eat," he says, pointing at my plate with his bread knife.

I pick up my fork again and nudge a slice of cucumber around the plate, then a wedge of tomato. When the phone finally rings, I bang my knee on the table jumping up to answer it.

"Hello?" I nearly shout.

"Molly. It's Katy."

I try to put a smile in my voice, to ward off any trouble. "Hi, Katy. How are you? I called back but you—"

"I know." A pause. "Molly, I have some bad news." And then, in a soft rush, she tells me that Joyce has died. How it happened has not been determined.

She was driving her blue Cadillac, possibly to the drugstore. It was ten-thirty at night. A gentle snow was falling. After stopping at a light, another driver reported, her car proceeded through the intersection, very slowly, before sideswiping three parked vehicles on the right. At that point it lost momentum and came to a stop. Joyce was unconscious, still holding the wheel, when they opened the door and got her out. She died on the way to the hospital.

It might have been her heart, Katy says, or a stroke. It might even have been a bad combination of drugs—she was taking pain medication.

"She was?"

"Oh, yes, for years. For her back. She had terrible disc pain from that accident with the Camaro."

This is news to me. Joyce never talked about her health, though I often shared my own dreary complaints: plantar fasciitis, bouts of eczema, gallbladder trouble. She'd always been sympathetic, I recall now, offering me bits of homey advice, remedies she'd heard or read about.

I start to ask too many questions then. Did she have a heart condition? Had she been ill? When would they have more information? Katy is hesitant, evasive, finally annoyed. She doesn't know, she says firmly; nothing is for certain. She will call me later, in a week or so. She'll let me know when the service will be held.

~

Doug is sitting on the sofa, his arms draped across the top of the cushions. He's not surprised, he says.

I look out the window at the bare branches of the maple tree, the blanched sky. "She was just here," I murmur, turning to face him.

"She should have taken better care of herself."

"It might have been a drug interaction, something she couldn't prevent."

"I doubt it."

So what? I am thinking. So what if she could have bought herself a couple more years? Joyce did what she wanted to do. While the rest of us were squaring off with life, Joyce was having a good laugh. Is laughing still, for all I know. The thought is something to cling to, a way to feel better. It isn't enough.

I keep seeing her car, in slow motion, cruising through that intersection. Soundlessly it crashes into the other cars, shudders to a stop. Snow is falling on the windshield. I cannot see Joyce inside.

"I can't stand not knowing what happened," I say suddenly, fiercely. "I need to know. I owe it to her."

"You don't owe her anything," Doug says. "She died. Knowing how it happened isn't going to change anything. Let it be."

"I can't," I tell him, and before he can say whatever it is he is bound to say, I walk out of the room. Right now I can't stand the sight of him.

He could have at least pretended to care—he didn't even hug me. With Joyce gone, Doug and I are left with each other. I suppose we had it coming.

~

I think of her far more now than I did when she was alive. I see her in sliding images, one frame after another, Joyce through the seasons of her life. The clarity of these pictures is astonishing.

Considering the scant attention I paid her, the miles between us, I don't know why I'm feeling so lost. It occurs to me that Joyce's affection, the rock-solid way she loved people, amounted to clemency. Without it, I have less hope for myself.

While my world feels different now, things at the nursery haven't changed. No matter what the odds, people bet on life. Yesterday the

Grave Digger, excited anew, made off with yet another doomed plant, this time a lovely young camellia. I wanted to save it, but who am I to thwart such eagerness?

# Archaeology After Dark

That's it for me," Roy announced, as he did every night.

Doris kept eying her cards.

"You're going to stay for a while?"

"For a while," she said. Why did he ask? Did she ever leave this early? And why did he bother to come here at all? He hated the noise and the smoke.

The queen of spades, reproachful, kept her gaze averted; she wanted no part of this. Doris sighed and glanced at her husband. His broad face loomed above her. His watery blue eyes regarded her kindly.

"I won't be long," she said, knowing this wasn't necessarily true and knowing it didn't matter: He would forgive her.

"Have fun," he said. "I'll meet you back at the room."

"See you soon," Doris murmured. She wondered if, with a queen and a seven, she should go for another card.

He patted her shoulder and walked away.

"Hit me," she commanded.

~

She never really enjoyed herself until after Roy left. Even if he was at a slot machine at the other end of the room, she could feel his devotion wafting her way, settling over her shoulders like a shawl. This wasn't the time or the place for that kind of encumbrance; this was supposed to be a free zone.

Already the lights seemed brighter, the laughter more boisterous. Doris swallowed the last of her Manhattan and gestured to the waitress with her empty glass. No problem getting service here—the staff wove through the crowd continually, bringing drinks, changing bills, guiding the elderly to the ATMs. They would trot out plates of food from the twenty-four-hour kitchen; they would guard the machines while patrons rushed to the restrooms; they would do even more if they only knew what.

Edie, the most cautious player at the table, was tonight's big winner. Grace had just finished her fourth vodka gimlet and was losing gleefully. Her husband kept closing his eyes and nodding off, and every few minutes Grace would look at him and shriek, "Time to put Ed to bed!" Next to them sat Evelyn, for whom a game of cards was no laughing matter.

They were all members of The Group, as they called themselves—a dozen or so fossil enthusiasts who assembled periodically for field trips. This time they were in Hawthorne, Nevada, looking for Cretaceous ammonites. As most of these ventures took place in the Nevada desert, they often stayed at motels with casinos, and, after a day scouring the rocky canyons, it was customary to gather in the evening at a card table.

Doris, at forty-eight, was the youngest member; most of them were over sixty. Happily retired, they drove up in old vans and dented trucks, vehicles sacrificed to the dusty pursuit of prehistoric treasure. Edie, who owned a vintage pickup much praised for its stamina, had surprised everyone by pulling into Hawthorne in a brand-new motor home. *What happened to the Ford?* they all wanted to know. Edie shook her head. *Had to shoot it.*

The dealer slid another card to Doris. She lifted one corner and winced. A king. She should be playing poker.

"I'm out," she said.

"Again?" said Edie. "Honey, you gotta learn to say no."

Everyone roared at this. Doris gave a shrug and reached for her cigarettes. She didn't care about winning; she simply wanted to be in this loud, bright room for as long as she could.

Leaning back in her chair, Doris turned to the left, and her body stiffened. In the glow of the slot machines, she caught a glimpse of brilliant white hair. But it wasn't him. Roy did not own a green plaid sport coat. And he would never, ever wear yellow cowboy boots.

Roy was meticulous about his appearance. You wouldn't catch him at the supermarket in a pair of old sweatpants and sneakers. Even here in the desert, he managed to keep his shirts crisp, his trousers creased. Back home, sometimes Doris would slide open the drawers of his stern mahogany highboy and gaze at the tidy array of socks, the neatly folded sweaters. When had he become so fastidious?

She looked down at her own outfit with detached curiosity: faded work shirt (minus a cuff button), limp cotton slacks. Everyone else, she noticed now, had changed for dinner.

Edie yawned and got to her feet. "I'm buying breakfast," she said, sweeping an armful of chips into her plastic container. Taking heed, the rest of the group began to gather their money and cigarettes. It was eleven o'clock, a sensible time to leave. Knowing Doris would stay longer, Edie laid a blue-veined hand on her shoulder.

"We're headed for Hollow Canyon tomorrow. It's a two-hour ride, bumpy as hell." She paused. "Aren't you tired, darlin'?"

"Not yet," Doris replied. Wise Edie nodded and said nothing more. Doris watched them file out. Only she and Earl remained at the table. Earl was not a member of the group. He was a local, the owner of a hardware store, and this was the third night in a row he had joined their party. From across the table, he gave her a winning smile and suggested they move into the bar.

~

Quarter after midnight. The roulette wheel spun, people cheered, bells rang on a slot machine. Out there, hungry coyotes jogged through the dark; here, it was as festive as Christmas.

Doris put a cigarette to her lips, and Earl snapped open his lighter, an old silver Zippo, chunky and reassuring. His hand was warm and heavy on her thigh, and she regarded it with interest, as if it had just arrived, as if it were sitting there all by itself, unattached to Earl. The long tan fingers fastened to her leg reminded her of a starfish. Gradually, like the approach of a distant train, the danger dawned on her: Someone might see them, a lingering member of the group. She looked at the people milling about, and her gaze fixed on a camera mounted near the ceiling—those black lenses were everywhere; they were probably under the tables. Right now, someone could be watching the progress of Earl's hand on television.

Or maybe Roy himself would wander in, sleepless and missing her. Would he say anything? She didn't think so. She had yet to find the borders of his tolerance.

He had been this way for nearly two years, ever since he came back. She still didn't know where he had spent those ten weeks after Toby died: She never asked. It was monstrous, her friends whispered, to leave her like that, only days after the funeral—and perhaps they were right, but the truth was, she had hardly noticed he was gone. She'd spent that time curled up on the end of the sofa, staring at the blue trail of cigarette smoke that spiraled into the lampshade beside her.

Although she couldn't remember much from that period, she could still see Roy's face when he told her he had to leave. His eyes, wide and sick with grief; tears rolling down his red cheeks. He kept seeing Toby, he said—every time he looked at her, he saw Toby. She had made no reply to this, had merely watched him leave. She did register a faint wave of shock, maybe even anger, but the feelings came from a faraway place, as if part of her had sheared off and was stranded somewhere. Even now she would look at her husband, at his tired eyes or the mosaic of broken veins in his cheeks, and a vague tenderness would come over her, like a scent through a window, and she would remember that on some disparate plane she still loved him.

Unlike Roy, Doris was not haunted by Toby's image, though it was true they bore a remarkable resemblance to each other. From her he had gotten his lean frame, blond hair, gray eyes, and rather large nose; the wide, crooked smile was hers as well. In the first few weeks after his death, she kept searching her face in the mirror, trying to catch sight of him. She would pause on the stairs, listening, waiting, as if she could breach his world by staying perfectly still. But the space around her was empty, vacant as a crater on the moon. He was gone from the rooms, gone from the mirrors, banished even from his photographs. They were eerie now, portentous. Pictures of a dead boy.

~

Doris placed a hand on Earl's wrist and leaned toward the wide yellow flame; she was growing very fond of that lighter. He lived nearby, he was telling her, two blocks away; they could walk there. Over the rim of her glass, she studied the rugged planes of his face and thought how pointless it was to be handsome in a place like Hawthorne.

She knew what his house would look like; she had walked down the rows of white boxes with their dirt yards and chain-link fences and green fiberglass carports. She imagined his bed, too large for the room, one side pushed against a wall. In the backyard, tethered to a slab of cement, a dog would be pacing. Every few minutes it would sigh and lie down.

Earl's hand squeezed her leg just a little. "You're a good-looking woman, you know that?"

Doris considered. A good-looking woman. No, she had no opinions about this.

"You are," he insisted, nodding his head. "Kind of skinny, but I like that."

He was wearing, Doris noticed, a class ring. At his age. A small gust of interest roused her, and she said, "You've been here all your life?"

"Nope. I grew up in Sparks. Came here"—he rubbed his jaw, reflecting—"twelve years ago."

"Why?" was all she could think of to say.

He shrugged. "It's cheap. Can't beat the price of homes here." He leaned toward her, leering in a friendly fashion. "You want to see mine? It's no palace, but it's paid for."

Doris heard the echo in that last line, and she knew it was one of his favorites.

There was no risk involved: She would get away with it. She would slip out of Earl's bed and back into Roy's, and her secret would perish in the desert. People weren't punished for their sins. Punishment came willy-nilly, despite faith or precaution or good deeds.

~

Toby was twenty-six the day he died. He'd been rock climbing, and something had gone wrong—something had come undone. He didn't suffer, they told her; he fell from a great height, and his death was quick. Doris could not envision this violent, sudden demise. She saw him toppling slowly, with amazement, the sky and rocks and trees whirling around him. To Toby, the fall must have seemed never-ending.

Doris had never wanted to be a mother, had sensed the danger early on. All through her only pregnancy, she worried that she wasn't fit for the task. Certain mammals, she had heard, would sometimes refuse their maternity, would shrink in terror from their young—a phenomenon she didn't find the least bit surprising.

~

One o'clock in the morning. Earl was getting a little bleary-eyed. He was a collector, too, he told her. He'd found all sorts of weird stuff in the desert. She should see some of the stuff he'd found. His hand, hot and damp on her thigh, waited for an answer.

Doris blew a stream of smoke out the side of her mouth. She pictured them in bed, their limbs entwined, their bodies straining in the moonlight. The image made her shudder.

The last time had been—what, a year ago? Longer. Roy had been very careful, had searched her face for signs of distress, had held his breath as he touched her—and, slowly, like ice breaking on a pond, she had responded. She clung to him, astonished, and he smiled down at her with such gratitude that she had to look away. And she noticed then how thin her arms had become, how pale his skin, and as their bodies began to move in rhythm, a terrible sadness welled up in her: They could not do this; they were still broken. "I can't," she whispered. "I'm sorry." He had not approached her since.

~

Earl wanted to know what kind of rocks her group was looking for.

"Fossils," said Doris. "Ammonites." She drew a spiral in the air with her finger.

Oh, yeah, he nodded, he had some of those, he had lots of rocks. But she should see the *bones* he'd found. He had seventeen steer skulls, most of them without any bullet holes, and a snake skeleton with *two heads*. Swear to God. People got a big kick out of that snake—this week he had it coiled around the sugar bowl.

Behind her glass, Doris grimaced. She could see herself an hour from now stumbling toward his bathroom, her hands groping for a light switch and finding some animal part tacked to the wall.

Roy wouldn't see any humor in a two-headed snake; the sight of it would probably pain him. He would make a special box for it, would treat it like a totem. She thought of the beautiful maple cabinets he had built to house their fossils; the weekends he had spent milling, sanding, and varnishing; and all the small moral debts he imposed on himself, the research and the data cards he compiled for every specimen. These things still mattered to him; he seemed, in fact, more scrupulous than ever.

She remembered the Shasta trip, when she and Roy had labored side by side on a rocky outcrop. They were a mile in the sky, and the wind blew cool on their skin as they swung their hammers and broke open chunks of limestone, grinning and sweating, shouting in triumph over each new find. He had not lost that exuberance, while she, who had spurred his interest in the hobby, who had found her first fossil at the age of six, was beginning to wonder if maybe they had enough of them.

~

Quarter to two.

"How about a nightcap?" Earl said, signaling the waitress. Doris opened her mouth to say no and then didn't bother.

He was divorced, he mentioned again. Three kids. Did she have kids? Doris shook her head. He paused, drummed his fingers on the table. Out of ideas, he winked and gave her another huge smile.

~

What was it Roy had said this morning? Something about a trip to Canada. Oh, yes—the dinosaur park. Was it next month they were going? He was the one who arranged these things.

He had sold his construction company last year and invested the considerable profits; presently he did consulting work, helping other business owners out of the red. Nothing could be drearier, Doris thought, than examining financial statements, but Roy never complained about it, and she wondered now, swirling the ice in her glass, if it soothed him. A red pencil, a sheet of paper. All those small repairs.

On this trip, he had brought along several home-and-garden magazines. He wanted to build a modest deck and was trying to come up with design ideas, but the more pictures he saw, the more elaborate his visions grew. His latest whimsy was a water garden. *We could put it beside the bedroom window*, he'd mused. *We could put a fountain in it and listen to the water.*

Doris had leaned back in the hotel bed and pictured this water garden. Murky water. Sluggish orange fish. The constant buzz of the pump.

*What do you think?* he asked, showing her a picture of an exquisite rectangular pool surrounded by glossy plants; a cougar made of stone was crouched nearby. You'd be filling it every two minutes, she was tempted to say, and you can't grow those plants in Sacramento. But what did it matter? Let him build his water garden. *It's pretty*, she said, and nodded.

How did he manage to keep making plans? From where did he wrest the interest? It wasn't just his projects he enjoyed—the smallest things stirred him: clouds, spiderwebs, palm fronds moving in the wind. Something had happened to him those ten weeks he was gone. There was a quietness about him now, a painstaking quality; she could see it in his hands, in the way he buttoned a shirt.

And just then, staring at the white webbing on the red candle holder on the bar, she understood: Roy was trying to save himself. He was trying to climb out of grief the way people ascend from madness: one fragile achievement at a time.

And though she hadn't helped him, not once in all these months, he was still waiting for her.

~

It was 2:05 a.m. Earl tilted the candle back and forth; with a tiny hiss, the flame went out. "Whoops," he said.

Doris looked at his perfect jaw, his bronze-colored skin, the creases around his eyes. Earl, encouraged by this scrutiny, moved his hand higher up her thigh and launched another oppressive grin. He leaned closer, so close that she could feel his breath on her cheek, and suddenly, more than anything in the world, she wanted to be with her husband. Setting down her drink, she grasped Earl's hand and placed it on his own thigh.

"Gotta go," she said.

Earl's face fell. "But—"

She got to her feet and walked unsteadily across the

blue-and-orange carpeting. It wasn't like jumping out of a plane—she could come back anytime. Still, she was afraid as she stepped outside the door and the dark pulled in around her. The night was cold, and it smelled of strange things. She glanced out into the desert, where only the stars could be seen, and there, maybe thirty feet away, a pair of yellow eyes appeared. They watched her a moment, and then they were gone.

# Waiting for Annie

I want to know why a thirty-five-mile-per-hour collision that left just a small blue welt on Annie's forehead has put her in a coma.

The doctor brightens at this, having been asked something he can answer. "It's a question of swelling," he says, uncapping his fountain pen and reaching for a pad of paper. With amazing speed he draws three profiles of a human head: erect, tilted forward, flung back. He is very good at this; he could make a living at it.

"When her head hit the steering wheel, the brain moved forward, hitting the front of the skull, and when her head went back, the brain bumped the back of the skull. The swelling developed from two places."

We talk about her brain, how when it swells there is no place for it to expand, and how this raises the intracranial pressure; as the pressure builds, the blood flow decreases, and the brain doesn't get enough oxygen. This makes sense to me, though I have never pictured Annie's brain as the spongy gray organ you see in science books.

The office is dimly lit, and instead of charts and X-rays there are pictures of national parks; even my chair is soft and considerate. We talk for almost an hour, about things that might or might not happen. The doctor is a mortal with red hair and fleshy, pockmarked cheeks, and I know I want too much from him. "Aside from monitoring pressure there's not much we can do," he admits. "We know so little about coma."

How many times has he spoken these words? How many people have sat in this chair, burdening him with their hopes? The skin droops around his sad blue eyes. You should have been an artist, I think as I close his office door.

I navigate toward Intensive Care, my terror of hospitals turning the corridors into eerie, aqueous chambers. Twice I get confused and have to ask one of the floating white coats to help me. At last I arrive, and for a moment I stand outside the glass doors, reluctant to enter this grim science project, this vault of dormant lives.

At least Annie can breathe on her own. They call this the *vegetative state*, which means I should not become overly excited when she twitches, coughs, or moans, as these actions can be reflexive. I look at the narrow bruise on her forehead, more noticeable against her pallor. Her deep-set eyes are closed, her mouth slightly open. I wipe some spittle from her chin and smooth her hair back from her face. "Annie," I say, a greeting and a test.

There is a bolt-like apparatus on her head where they have stuck in a tiny tube that checks the pressure inside. I am told this causes no harm as they send this device into the "silent part" of the brain where no important functions take place. Nothing seems more fantastic to me— that they can pilot this thing in between her circuitry. There is tubing in her nose, as well as her arms, and some kind of sensor is attached to her earlobe. She is, at the moment, more machine than person.

She makes a sound, and I jump. "Annie," I urge. I reach for her hand, squeeze it. Her fingers are cool and remote. I tuck her arms closer to her sides and pull the sheet higher.

A nurse comes up behind me. "Time to leave, honey."

I give her a nod and take a last look at Annie, my long-limbed broken doll.

~

Last night I spent wedged on an orange vinyl couch in the hospital lounge. Scattered around me were other wakeful souls too distraught over their loved ones to attempt conversation. Now, driving back home to Berkeley, I pass by the bay without bothering to look at it. My eyes burn, and my unwashed face feels as if it's covered with a fine web. Drivers are frowning, zipping by me. There is no sympathy on the open road.

Over and over I force those drawings on myself. Brain hitting bone, forward, then back.

All that Annie is—every gesture, quirk, and mood—has become two and a half pounds of damaged tissue.

~

I push open the front door, and the cats rush in ahead of me. Hungry, winding around my legs, they have no time for my grief. As soon as I fill their bowls, they turn their backs on me.

After I check the phone (there are no messages from the hospital), I can't think what to do. There is probably mail in the box, though I see no point in getting it. The lamps and furniture, the pictures on the wall—nothing seems familiar or significant. I go back to the kitchen and scan the wall calendar, but the events—a play, a haircut, dinner at Chez Panisse—are inconceivable. A fear expands in my chest: the idea that I am not up to this, that I won't be able to manage the tasks expected of me. My heart begins to pound, and I look to the cats for help. One is washing her face and does not answer me; the other is on the sofa trying to sleep. When I call her name, she flicks her tail in warning.

Taking deep breaths, I try to remember my role in all this, the papers I need to locate, the people I need to call. Annie's mom— she's the first. Again I dial the number, and again there is no answer. This is the number she gave us six months ago, but the operator tells me there is no Key West listing for a Ms. Janet LaMarche. Which is no surprise: Annie's mother has had at least eight addresses in as many years, and some of these were boats. I am not well acquainted with Janet, having seen her only twice, but I know she's not big on sentiment—holidays pass without a word from her. Strangely, Annie doesn't seem to mind: They must have an understanding, a pact I'm not privy to. While Annie describes her mother as "exotic," I employ a different word, one I keep to myself.

Tomorrow Kerry flies in from Colorado. I have not seen him in a year and a half, since he left us to live with his father. I like to evoke the child version of him, the towheaded four-year-old who took his world on trust. Our first year together was a state of grace: Annie and I were head over heels, still getting to know each other and adoring each new discovery, and in the bargain there was her child to love. I had never wanted children of my own, and the ease I felt with Kerry, the swiftness of my devotion, surprised me. As he grew older and began pulling away from us, groping for a life of his own, I braced myself for the changes I saw coming. It's not easy for two women to raise a boy, and while there was no real discord at home, I know there must have been awkwardness, maybe even trouble, at school. While I didn't fault Kerry for leaving us, the news came like a blow to the chest. I've never shared this hurt with him, nor am I likely to; if he harbors any resentment toward me—and he very well may—he has been equally discreet.

Rick is not coming; he is busy managing his steakhouse in Denver and wants to be "kept informed." We're not talking about an offshore hurricane, I wanted to say. Am I expecting too much? I know it's been eleven years since the divorce, and I know I'm the last person he wants to be in the same room with, but for Kerry's sake, if not Annie's, shouldn't Rick come along, at least for a day or two? The dearth of family appalls me. I think of Annie's errant mother; and her father, who was killed in a car wreck; and her sister, who died of cancer—all who have loved her and are not here.

I spend a long time on the phone, with friends, insurance agents, Annie's employer, my own. I say the same things so many times that the words become simple tools, stripped of feeling. Afterward I wander into the kitchen, open a can of tomato soup, and pour it unheated into a bowl. I am not hungry, but I feed myself anyway, swallowing the soup in small, steady spoonfuls, like medicine.

~

First by his walk, I recognize Kerry. He is taller, and his dark blond hair is now black. He keeps his head low as he lopes down the ramp, pretends he's not searching for me.

"Kerry!" I open my arms; he allows a brief hug before backing off. "Hey," he says.

I pat his leather back as we walk down the hall. "You've grown so tall!" I say, feebly. I am aghast, of course, at the black hair hanging in his face, the rips in his blue jeans, the heavy martial boots.

"How was your flight?"

He shrugs. "Boring."

"Well, that's probably a good thing." I'm hoping for a smile but don't get one.

"How's Mom?"

139

"I haven't heard from the hospital, so I guess there aren't any changes. We're headed there now."

In the car, I tell Kerry what happened. "She was driving on Grizzly Peak. A collie ran out, and when she swerved to miss it, she hit a tree."

I look at his profile, and my stomach flutters. He has Annie's long, straight nose; she's there in the set of his mouth, too.

For a moment he says nothing, and then, in a rush: "So what do they think—is she going to be okay?"

I put my hand on his arm. "They don't know, Kerry. But she is breathing on her own, which means that her brain stem is functioning, and they haven't had to drain off much fluid." I try to explain to him what I've learned about coma, but I see his discomfort and stop.

"I can't get through to your grandmother in Florida," I tell him. "Have you heard from her?"

Kerry snorts. "Not likely." He turns and looks out at the bay, green and rippling in the March wind. "You know she's fucking nuts."

~

I am fighting rising nausea. We are back in the slick halls of the hospital, and that smell—half sweet, half antiseptic—is following us.

"I hate these places," Kerry murmurs.

"You're not alone."

I try to prepare him for the sight of his mother. "She's hooked up to a lot of equipment."

"Duh."

*Oh, Kerry, please be nice.* We don't say another word until we walk into the ICU and approach Annie's bed. The circles under her

140

eyes are darker today. I check her heart rhythms on the monitor and let out my breath.

"Annie?" I try.

Kerry, whom I have forgotten, is pointing to the bolt in her head. "What's that?"

"It's for checking the pressure in her brain—it keeps her head steady."

His face starts to crumple. I put an arm around him, and he shakes it off.

"Talk to her," I say.

"Why?" he demands. "She can't hear me."

"Maybe she can."

"Mom," he says finally. "It's Kerry."

There is only the hum of the machines and her chest rising and falling. I lay my hand on her shoulder and bring my mouth close to her ear. "We're here, Annie," I whisper. Even her scent is missing.

~

He's not going back, Kerry tells me as we pull out of the parking lot. "What's the use?"

I do not tell him what I've heard: that talking to a coma patient might help, that the brain, acting on cue, working in the dark, may begin to heal itself in an attempt to answer.

"It's okay, Kerry. You don't have to."

Suddenly his fist slams the dashboard. *"Fucking dog!"*

~

This house seems too small for him now, or maybe it's his wrath the rooms can't contain. The cats, dismayed, have gone into hiding;

even I am disturbed by this strange male presence, so unlike the eager youth who once lived here. I watch him pick up the TV remote, slap it against his palm a few times, then smack it back down on the coffee table. What am I supposed to do with him?

"Come in here," I say. "Keep me company while I make us a sandwich."

Kerry tromps into the kitchen and yanks a chair out from the table.

"Why are you so mad?"

"She's just lying there," he snarls, "and no one's doing a fucking thing."

I keep my eyes on the bread I'm buttering. "For one thing," I tell him, "they are doing everything they can. And for another, I think you're wearing out that adjective."

He crosses his leg over his knee and starts tapping his fork against the heel of his boot.

I put the sandwich in the skillet and turn to face him. I know he's scared, I know that's why he's angry, but I can't do this.

"This is an awful time, Kerry—we have to help each other through it. I can't be fighting you right now."

He stops the fork, nods at the floor.

~

I slip into the cold expanse of the bed and contemplate Annie, trapped in some distant dimension. Her mind is still active, the doctor said; it just isn't communicating with her body. "In coma," he said, "the brain attempts to rewire itself to compensate for the damage." Which makes me think of science fiction movies: a brain with a life of its own.

I don't feel any anger; for me, there is just the waiting.

~

We met one morning at the store where I work, Set in Stone. We sell paving material for driveways and patios. I watched her pause before a display wall and consider the various options. She was wearing a green shirt, and her khaki pants were stuffed into her boots. She was gangly and unselfconscious, absorbed in the samples.

"Good morning," I said, approaching her. "Can I help you?"

She turned to me and smiled. "Hi." The first thing I noticed was her deep-set eyes—large, gray-blue, slightly crazed—and then her wide, easy grin. There was no discernible style to her blonde hair, which fell in loose coils around her face and neck. On her shirt and hands were small, colorful spatters of paint. "Is flagstone the best thing for patios?"

"It's a great look." I nodded. "There's no maintenance, and it's pretty easy to install."

"Do you have people who do that?"

I liked her voice, which was deeper than I expected, and friendly. "Sure. How big is the area?"

"Tiny," she said. "It's just a patch of dead grass right now."

"I could probably do it for you," I told her. "I could come out and give you a bid if you want."

"That would be super," she said. "Sooner the better."

I did this kind of side work from time to time, and so our beginnings were innocent enough. I probably should have packed up my tools and driven away, though, as soon as I started looking forward to those spring days in her Montclair backyard, when she would come outside and chat with me after working in her studio. (Annie is an artist. She creates the most wonderful canvases, not of scenery or figures but of colors, gorgeous, haunting colors that make you feel all sorts of things.) While I stretched string lines and arranged the pavers, we shared pieces of our pasts, who and what we admired, where we'd been or wanted to go. I loved the quickness of her mind, her far-ranging interests—how she didn't aim for cleverness or approval but spoke without artifice and maligned no one. Kerry, who was four then, would often dig in the dirt beside me. On the mornings he wasn't there, when his father took him on errands, Annie would sometimes light a joint, which we genially passed, and as I knelt in the soft earth, listening to her stories, watching her exuberant gestures, I let myself fall more deeply in love. If there was a key moment, a point at which I could have walked away, no harm done, I missed it. By the time I finally kissed her, right there under the sun, no force on earth could have stopped me.

The only thing Rick had given her was Kerry, which was all she'd wanted from him anyhow.

~

Tired of trying to sleep, I get up at 4:10 a.m. and hear faint laughter coming from the TV in Kerry's room. He doesn't answer when I tap on the door, so I turn the knob and take a look inside. He is lying on the bed, fully dressed and sound asleep. On the small, black-and-white screen, Lucy and Ethel are stuffing chocolates into their mouths. I watch them a moment, more comforted by their silliness than amused, before crossing the room and banishing them with a click. The screen crackles softly and goes blank.

I am sitting at the table stroking our cat Emma and staring at the pepper grinder when Kerry comes into the kitchen. He is subdued this morning, and Emma, who was ready to flee, settles back into my lap.

"You have any Coke or Pepsi?" he asks, and when I say no he surprises me by pouring a cup of coffee, which he modifies with milk and four spoonfuls of sugar.

"I called the sheriff in Key West," I tell him. "I'm having them look for your grandmother."

"Whatever." He stirs his coffee, and I notice the tattoo on his arm. It's a dark blue cockroach, about two inches long.

"Why a cockroach?" I ask him. I really want to know.

"It's the only thing that lasts," he says, defiant, tossing the hair out of his eyes. "Whatever you do to it, it survives."

"Was it painful?"

He shakes his head.

"They can take those off, can't they?"

"Who cares?"

*You will care*, I manage not to say. *When you are forty, you will care.* I wonder what Rick thinks of that tattoo—why, in fact, he allowed it; Kerry is still a minor.

"What are you going to do today?"

He stretches his long legs out in front of him and scratches his shoulder. "Guess I'll go up on Telegraph Avenue, see what the freaks are up to." He yawns then, and in his wrinkled brow I see a vestige of his childhood face. In ways that elude expression, in ways grown nearly useless, I know this boy; I carry his youth with me. Impossible, this new version of him: The dark trace of beard, the scatter of pimples, the sheer *size* of him astonishes me.

"Have I mentioned," I say, "how great it is to see you?"

Before he can stop himself, he grins.

~

The doctor is encouraged. They have removed the cranial bolt, as the pressure in her brain is returning to normal. She is also showing some "localized reactivity," and her pupils are contracting when light is shone on them. This is not a profound coma, the doctor adds, and there are many indications that point to recovery.

My heart is beating in my throat.

"She is responding to pain," he continues, "and she is starting to blink, signs that the cortex is waking up." But then he rubs his eyes with his meaty red hands, and I know there is something else he is obliged to tell me.

"It's important to remember," he begins, "that every brain is unique. Sometimes we expect the worst and are happily surprised; sometimes it works the other way." It's possible, he explains, that Annie could persist in a vegetative state, that she might be able to sleep and wake, to swallow and digest, without ever regaining consciousness.

This information seeps in slowly, horribly. I will not be free of it.

I tell him that I don't understand this, how someone can be both dead and alive.

He brings his hands together, palm to palm, and clears his throat. "The persistent vegetative state is a cessation of thinking," he says. "In PVS, the cortex is damaged, but the lower parts of the brain, the autoregulatory responses, still work. The body is kept alive." He gives a slight shrug. "With some help from us."

PVS. So it's common enough for an acronym.

"But let's not get ahead of ourselves," he says quickly. "The swelling was minor in Annie's case, and now it's gone. She is showing definite improvement."

I get to my feet, wobbly, and he rises from his own chair and places his hand on my back as he walks me out the door. "Try to be patient," he says. "Remember that the brain is always working on behalf of the organism. Protecting it."

I look at him askance. "So Annie's in a coma for her own good?"

"Essentially."

Organism. A week ago Annie was a person. I can't imagine seeing her that way—that simply—ever again. Even if she is fully restored, I can't imagine being able to forget this.

~

Today they let me spend a longer time with Annie than usual. Freed from the bolt and the nasal tubes, she looks almost normal, and for a few seconds I allow myself the fantasy that she will wake when I whisper her name.

Someone has placed a chair next to her bed, and obligingly I sit down. Picking up her hand, I tell her everything that comes to mind, and though she makes no sounds, twice I see her blink. I talk to her about Kerry and the cats, and just as I start to tell her about all the cards and flowers she's gotten, her mouth yanks down, and I see tears slide toward her temples. A moment later her expression is placid again.

I sprint out of the room and find a nurse.

"She just cried! She was crying!" The nurse, who remains calm, follows me back into the room. She checks the monitors, opens Annie's eyes and speaks her name, and then she turns to me and says, gently, "Sometimes they do that. It doesn't mean anything."

~

Kerry is hunched over the photo albums when I get home. He looks up at me, expectant, and I muster a cheerful tone.

"They think she might be waking up."

His eyes widen. "No kidding?"

"She's responding to certain tests, and they've taken some of the gadgets off her."

147

Kerry slaps his knee. "That is so great. So did she say anything?"

"Not yet," I say brightly.

He follows me into the kitchen. "I bought this for dinner." He opens the fridge and pulls out a large cheese pizza. "I was going to get pepperoni, but then I remembered you don't eat meat."

"How sweet. Thank you." I make him suffer a hug.

"Should we heat it up now?" he asks.

"Sure." We sit down at the kitchen table, me with my glass of wine and Kerry with a giant bottle of Coke. "I bought this, too," he says, lifting his drink. "Things cost more here than they do in Denver."

"Do you like it there?"

"It's all right. I skied a lot this winter."

"How's the restaurant business?"

"Pretty good, I guess. Dad's opening another one in August." This pleases me only insofar as it bodes well for Kerry's future. "He wants me to bus tables next winter, but I don't want to. I want a job at a ski resort—ever heard of Winter Park?"

I shake my head.

"It's huge," he says, throwing his arms apart. "A ton of trails. Me and my friend Ethan are going to rent a condo there and work the lifts. We can ski for nothing."

I lean back in my chair and listen as he tells me about his plans to join a ski patrol and learn rescue. He is talkative today, full of smiles, and I am delighted by this shift in his mood. Every so often one of Annie's expressions will cross his face, or his hands will move precisely like hers, and each time this happens I rejoice.

It is not until after dinner, when Kerry is watching television and I am washing dishes, that the fear moves back in. A deft shadow, it creeps up from behind, settles between my shoulders. I see myself feeding Annie, bathing her, rocking her—she is looking right through me; she is looking at nothing. I pull my hands from the water and grip the edge of the sink. A low wail escapes me.

"Jane?" Kerry says. I feel his hand on my shoulder. Awkwardly, he starts patting me. "It's okay, she's getting better. Don't cry," he pleads. And shamelessly, knowing he is not strong enough, I fall apart in his arms.

~

I wait in the hall as a physical therapist finishes working with Annie, manipulating her arms and legs to help preserve muscle tone. She has been moved to another wing of the hospital, one with pictures on the walls and fewer machines. Now she sleeps in a room with a window, surrounded by the flowers they disallowed in Intensive Care. I place some roses next to her bed, hoping the fragrance will find her.

Yesterday, when I was talking, she turned her head to me. Hearing, the doctor affirms, is the last sense to go and the first to return. She is also moving her limbs more, which is another good sign, but what we are waiting for is "perceptivity," something that can't be coincidence.

There is a bit of color in her cheeks now, and the shadows under her eyes are not as dark. I pull the chair close to the bed and watch the feelings that come and go on her face. Sometimes her eyebrows will rise as if she's surprised; sometimes she will scowl—but what I witness most often, what pulls me to my feet, is her mask of anguish. Whenever I see that grimace, I picture her brain as a labyrinth of bad dreams, a reddish-black netherworld through which she is stumbling.

Never does she smile.

~

The house is reclaiming me. I am watering plants, filling bird feeders, scouring stains from the sink. I accomplish these tasks unwittingly, as if a part of me, aware of what must be done, is stepping in.

Some things in the house do capture my interest: Annie's paintings. I find myself contemplating them for long moments. My favorite is a canvas she calls "Day Break." Gradations of deep blue on top, dark green on the bottom, and a pencil-thin layer of brilliant orange in between. The effect is stunning.

"Do you see the paintings in your mind," I once asked her, "before you start? Or do they surprise you?"

She'd concentrated a moment. "I do see them first. I have this idea, and then the colors take over for me."

All these new circuits the doctor speaks of, this re-wiring that is going on while Annie sleeps—what will it mean to her art? Will she want to paint the same way? Will the colors be as lovely?

Will she want to paint at all?

~

Running errands, I stop at Seconds on Shattuck and speak with Annie's employer, a portly man with florid cheeks and kind eyes. Annie, who adores vintage clothes, makes quite a lot of money mending them. She has worked for James for more than six years, and he has been good to her in many ways—we stay in his condo whenever we visit Lake Tahoe. Now he stands before me, asking about Annie and wringing his hands. I tell him the signs are promising, and in a rush of emotion he hugs me hard. Then he clasps my hands between his own and tells me that he is here for me, that if there is anything he can do for me, anything at all, please let me know.

The same thing happens when I stop at Set in Stone. The owner is there, covering for me, and with teary eyes she tells me that she wants to help in whatever way she can. Our friends are behaving in similar fashion, though everyone is hesitant, circumspect, not wanting to ask too many questions or offer reassurance they might wish they hadn't.

Kerry and I sit on the deck after lunch, watching a pair of yellow finches peck at the feeder. Annie's red tulips nod in the breeze, and the astilbe is pushing its soft stems skyward. Even as we speak, the magnolia unfurls its slick pink petals. Spring is gaining momentum.

Worried that Kerry is growing restless, I tell him I will understand if he wants to head back to Colorado. "You can come back when she wakes up." I always use the word *when*, not *if*, in my conversations with Kerry. "It might take a while," I add. "No one knows."

He shakes his head. "No. I want to stay."

I look out at the tulips, bending so easily, and tell him what the doctors have told me: that Annie will not wake up like people do in the movies. That she will have to relearn things, that this will take time.

He narrows his eyes, processing this information, then folds his arms on the table and says, "So I'll help."

I have doubts about a fifteen-year-old boy caring for his mother in this fashion—I have doubts about my own ability—but I don't share them. I look at his profile, so young, so dogged, and what I say is, "Thank you."

Kerry shrugs and, keeping his eyes averted, says, "I'd do the same for you, if you were the one who got hurt."

Gratitude takes my breath away. I can't speak. This keeps happening, this overwhelming thankfulness I feel when someone is kind to me. Even a smile from an unknowing shop clerk brings me to my knees.

~

The next day Kerry comes to the hospital with me. From the folder he's carrying, I see he has a plan. We pause at the door to Annie's room, which is partly open, and slowly he leans in and looks at his mother. The folder in his hand is shaking.

I look at the monitors, as I do every time. Green numbers on a black screen, changing subtly, and a graph at the bottom, the translation of her heart. I don't know what all these numbers mean—seeing them is enough.

Annie is very still today. I lower my eyes to the sheet on her chest, wait for the rise and fall. Has she lost ground? Those promising signs—were they misleading? I think of what the doctor said the first time we spoke. *We know so little about coma.*

"How does she look?" Kerry whispers.

"Fine," I tell him, "and you don't have to whisper—it's better if we don't."

He nods knowingly. "That's why I brought this." He opens the folder and takes out a few sheets of paper. "It's something I had to write for biology class. It's about bees. You know how Mom loves them."

She does. We have rusty garden art in the shape of bees, and there are several photographs in the house: bees among the lavender stalks, bees in the yellow centers of Shasta daisies—close-ups that Annie took in the garden. This report must be something Rick sent him, along with his school books; his teachers are giving him assignments, work he can do to keep from falling too far behind.

So we sit down next to her bed, and Kerry reads his report on bee colonies and why they are in trouble. Fascinated, I listen so closely that at first I don't see the arm that Annie has raised. Kerry stops reading, and we both stare at her arm, waiting for it to do more. Slowly it descends to the sheet.

"What does *that* mean?" Kerry says, his voice thick with excitement.

"Hard to say. But I think it's a good thing."

~

Two days later, two weeks after the accident, Annie looks at me. Not long, maybe four seconds, but I know her eyes, and I know she was there.

Her doctor was right. People don't wake up as you might guess. It happens fitfully, one false start after another. Annie is full of surprises that first week. One moment she is lying there, and the next she is sitting. Several times she throws off the sheets and walks stiff-legged around the bed. Occasionally she answers a question, and occasionally I can make sense of it.

The doctor is exultant. He is in here every chance he gets, demonstrating ways I can help her. The learning is slow. Over and over, I show her how to dress, how to use a fork and knife, how to brush her teeth. There may be lingering problems, the doctor cautions: lowered stress tolerance, delayed responses, sluggish abstract reasoning. "A full recovery," he says, "may take months." At last, they let me bring her home.

~

Because she has trouble enunciating, because she often puts words in the wrong places and calls her belt "that round cow thing," a speech therapist comes twice a week, along with a physical therapist and a neuropsychologist who charts her cognitive achievements. We are all pitching in to rebuild her.

Good to his word, Kerry is helping, more than I could have guessed, and not just with errands and housework. At first he hung back, alarmed by his mother's faltering progress, but then he began watching the therapists, learning from them, and by now he is invaluable: I do not believe she'd be doing this well without him. And with a job to replace his anger, Kerry has benefitted, too. Another piece of good news: Janet has been found. She was sailing with friends off the coast of Venezuela and will be here by the weekend.

Yes, Annie is coming along. Soon Kerry will be leaving, and I will head back to work, and Annie will take up where she left off. It will be some time before she starts mending garments again—her hands are not altogether dependable yet—but she has already begun to paint.

Last night she was at her easel, mixing shades of blue, her hand moving tentatively. After a moment she paused and regarded the empty canvas. I interrupted then, asked her if she saw the pictures in her head the way she used to. She looked up from the palette and smiled at me. "Yes. Why?"

She has no recollection of the accident or her coma, and she is fascinated by my account of her ordeal. "I cried?" she says, incredulous. To her, it's just a story. She can't imagine how far she's traveled, the terrible journey behind her smile.

# Double Take

At the age of two you were wearing glasses, light blue frames with butterflies on the corners. Behind the thick lenses your eyes were enormous, and when you peered up at people on the street, they stopped and beamed at you; they couldn't help it. That wispy blonde hair. Those glasses.

Some say we all have a double. Today I think I met yours. She was sitting on the curb, engrossed in a book she held close to her face. I softened at the sight of her, at the capacity of children to lose themselves in smaller worlds, for there were cars going by and dogs barking and a skateboarder rocketing down the sidewalk. As I got closer I noticed the blue glasses, the blonde tangle of curls. My stomach jumped. She had your fair skin and red cheeks; she had your *overbite*. I stopped and stared, and when she finally looked at me, her forehead wrinkling just like yours, it was all I could do not to rush over and hug her. I stood there grinning, widely, helplessly.

"What are you reading?" I blurted.

Sheets of light slid across her glasses as she appraised me. She looked about eight years old.

"*The Boxcar Children*," she said, showing me the cover. "It's the one where they save the animals."

"Who are the Boxcar Children?" I asked, stalling.

"They used to live in a boxcar," she explained with exaggerated patience. "But now they live with their grandfather, and they solve mysteries."

You're not going to believe this, Bett—she had a scar on her chin, not quite where yours is, but *my God.*

I didn't think twice. I sat right down on the curb and helped myself to her day. Had she been even a year older she might have resisted, might have dismissed me with a single scornful look, but I could see she was not done with childhood, had not yet lost that hopeful curiosity.

Her parents had named her Ginger, after the movie star. This threw me. "Ginger Rogers?" I asked. She shook her head. "Ginger from *Gilligan's Island*. The movie star." And that's not all. She has a sister called Margarita—named after her mother's favorite drink.

I asked her where she lived, and she pointed to the building behind us, one of those ratty duplexes. I could hear a television blaring; someone was watching a game show. There were two large clay pots on the porch; a dingy white cat languished in one, and the other held a dead ficus. In the skeleton of its branches a bald, naked Barbie hung by one arm. I looked at the litter caught in the shrubs, and the packed dirt yard studded with yellow weeds, and the tower of used tires stacked against the house, and I could understand how the people inside might name their daughter after a character in a TV show.

You kept appearing—in the line of her jaw, in the way her upper lip edged over the lower—and each time I saw you, a thrill ricocheted through me. I was having a good time, Bett. I couldn't see any harm in pretending.

However much Ginger resembles you, her personality is altogether different. She's very serious. I can't imagine her slipping Oreos behind her glasses and waiting for the teacher to notice. The things you got away with! Not through guile—you simply wanted to entertain. And people sensed this; they let you disarm them. Barbara and I couldn't figure it out, how you invited trouble and never got into it. Most sisters would have been jealous; I guess you charmed us, too.

In temperament Ginger seems more like me. A ferocious nail biter, for one thing. I bet she goes to pieces over the slightest setback. She showed me some of the schoolwork she had tucked into her book, and everything had a gold star pasted on it. Remember those stars, what a big deal they were? On second thought, you probably don't remember; you never needed that sort of validation. (Did you, by the way, ever get any of those stars?)

We talked for more than two hours. Her mother sells makeup, she told me, and her father "fixes things."

"Like what?" I said.

She shrugged. "Cars. Toasters, too." She squinted at the duplex. The sounds of a ball game could now be heard. I frowned at the open window and looked back at Ginger. Her green plaid dress hung off her shoulders; the hem had fallen in a couple places, and there was a rip alongside the zipper. Her bare feet rested on the oily asphalt. I wanted to see her in a T-shirt and blue jeans and brand-new red sneakers.

I told her I'd stop by tomorrow to give her some books to read, and I was alarmed by the way her face lit up. Already she is counting on me.

When I reached the end of the block, I looked back. She was staring after me. Dogs do that—watch you leave them behind. She's a stray I shouldn't have petted. Now her need has followed me home, is waiting outside my door.

Maybe, after you, I have no reserves left, no space to harbor another soul. You never knew, did you, the extent of my dedication, the lengths I went to foster you? You were busy taking care of yourself. What daring you showed, tossing aside rules, ignoring boundaries, fashioning a childhood you could move around in. Although you could manage your schoolwork with ease, you often shunned it just for the fun of forging a good note: *Dear Mrs. Drew, Bett couldn't do her homework last night because our furnace broke and her hands got too cold*; or, *Bett is late today because her grandmother forgot to take her medicine and had to be rushed to the hospital.* People loved that excess in you. Later, your tales became more extravagant, your maneuvers more evasive, and still no one thought to be concerned.

How did you do it? How did you slip away while everyone was watching?

~

Ginger was waiting for me in the same spot I'd left her, wearing the same green dress. The sun shone through her curls and reflected off her glasses, and again I felt that yearning, that pointless elation. *You look just like my little sister*, I wanted to explain, though what could she say to that? This was a situation neither of us could help.

I sat down on the curb. She hugged her knees and grinned at me. She had teeth like a doll's, small and square and very white, with slivers of space in between. Astonished, I grinned back. Had anyone ever looked at me with such patent delight?

A blanket of June heat hung over the neighborhood. Ginger's hair stuck to her forehead in tiny golden rings; it could stand to be washed, I noticed, as could her nails, which were etched with crescents of dirt. I did a little sleuthing, asked what she ate for dinner last night, and she told me she had a cheese sandwich. "I made it myself," she added.

"Oh?" I said, all innocence. "Your mom lets you make your own dinner?"

Ginger nodded vigorously. "She *likes* me to."

A black lab came panting up to us. Tongue lolling, he sniffed our knees and jogged on. Ginger didn't seem the least bit afraid of him; she was eying the books I had brought. "You can read these two yourself," I said, handing her my tattered hardback copies of *Heidi* and *Black Beauty*. "And this one I'll read to you." I showed her the cover. "*Charlotte's Web*. Do you know the story?"

She shook her head.

"Well, it's about a spider and a pig."

"I don't like spiders."

"You'll like this one."

Raising my voice above the thumping music of car radios, above the children shrieking through sprinklers, I read the first four chapters. I kept expecting her to interrupt, to argue with the author like you always did, but she was very quiet. A couple times she tapped my arm and asked me to read a sentence again, and when I did, she listened closely, nodding and smiling to herself. I don't know why she did this—whether she didn't understand the first time or whether she just liked hearing the words.

Just as I began to tell Ginger I had to be going, her mother drove up in an old, light blue Ford Galaxie. She did not greet her daughter, nor did Ginger acknowledge her, but it was clear enough who she was. Ginger and I watched as she swung out of the car, slammed the door, and headed for the duplex. She's a tall woman, rake-thin, with straggly red hair and skin so pale I could see the veins in her legs. A pack of Kools stuck out of the front pocket of her shorts. Halfway to the porch she glanced over at us, and her steps slowed a fraction. She eyed me with a mixture of mistrust and confusion. What was this grown woman doing sitting on the curb with her daughter?

For a moment I thought she might stop, but her desire to avoid us was stronger. With a warning scowl, she turned her back and hurried to the front door.

~

There are four trees on Ginger's block, four scabby sycamores planted by the city. Imagine growing up without woods or meadows. Where does she go for solace?

Remember in the winter how we'd strip the boughs off pines and weave them into forts? The snow would fall down the back of our necks and our mittens would freeze and we'd have to stamp our feet against the cold, and still we hunkered inside those green walls. They were *ours,* those frozen oases; inside them, safe as unmapped treasure, we had power.

Sometimes I think you're still building those forts, the way you move from town to town, from cabins to trailers to rooms for rent. Occasionally you'll send postcards, which I pin to my wall and use to track you. Now you're in Virginia, living on the edge of a lake. "Someone's summer cabin," you wrote. Tell me what it looks like—I need to see you in it; I need to fix you in time. Right now I imagine you sitting in the kitchen, your arms folded across a speckled Formica table; you're gazing through the screen door at a butterfly perched on some Queen Anne's lace; its black and yellow wings close and open, close and open.

Yesterday I brought Ginger to my apartment: She wanted to see my tropical fish. I didn't have to ask her parents—they weren't home. It was so easy, Bett. She just took my hand, and off we went. I am afraid for her.

I live only seven blocks from Ginger, but there are trees in my neighborhood—grand trees, spreading over rooftops, shading the whole street. When I lie in bed I can look up into the branches of a huge cedar. Sometimes I'll find a squirrel or blue jay staring at me.

"What's that one?" she asked, putting a grubby finger on the side of the aquarium.

"A neon tetra."

"What's that one?"

"A bleeding heart."

"A *bleeding heart?*" she echoed, bringing her face close to the tank, trying to see this gruesome phenomenon.

There you were again, in her profile, your forehead scrunched in concentration, your lips pursed with wonder. "Give me your glasses a minute," I said. "They're covered with fingerprints." Obediently she handed them over, and for the first time I saw her whole face, disarmed, helpless. No longer able to see the fish, she turned away from the tank and simply waited, her gaze suspended and peaceful.

She liked the sunken ship and the way the fish swam through a hole in its side. I told her about the otters in Monterey Bay and how they wrap themselves in kelp before they fall asleep, and the sea turtles that swim through the green depths of the ocean, day and night, for hundreds and hundreds of miles, to lay their eggs on a special island.

"How do they find it?" she whispered in awe.

"Nobody knows," I whispered back.

Ginger's father was in the driveway when we returned. Abruptly Ginger let go of my hand; I could feel her stiffen beside me. Shirtless, hunched behind the raised hood of the Galaxie, he straightened up and stared at us. I could see each one of his ribs and a long scar that started near his breastbone and ended somewhere below his belt. His hands were black with oil.

"Where *you* been?" he said, his voice snide, accusing.

"We took a walk," I said quickly, edging in front of Ginger. "I live up on Ellsworth—I showed Ginger my tropical fish."

He rolled his eyes at this and turned back to the car. I walked over to him. He had some kind of cyst on his shoulder; it stuck out like an egg.

"My name is Lorrie Thayer."

"Yeah, I know about you," he said, peering at the engine. "Why are you hanging around Ginger?"

"I like her."

He snorted. "Well, I think it's weird." He picked up a long wrench and began loosening a bolt. I watched the tendons moving in his forearms. There was no way out of it; I had to appease him. So I apologized. Next time, I told him, I'd ask his permission. He didn't say a word, but I did get a nod out of him.

He gives me the creeps. That hard nub of a chin, the way his pants hang on his hip bones, the look on Ginger's face when she saw him: not quite fear; not hatred, either—she's still too young to hate. It was a look of dread.

What can be more dreadful than childhood? Old age, maybe. Either way, you're doomed to submission. Though at least when you're old, no one wants to touch you.

Of course I suspect him.

~

I almost bought you a book the other day, and then I realized: You probably don't read much anymore—not books, anyway. You probably can't even sit through a movie. You were such an ardent reader. I wonder if you miss it, if you remember the way you used to be, if you remember anything at all.

Now I see you walking in the tall, wet grass along the lake, scaring small frogs into the water. A loon calls out; you search the still, black surface but can't see it. Darkness is coming, creeping in around the trees; the crickets, impatient, have already started. Chilled, you shove your fists deeper into your pockets and head for the yellow light of the porch.

~

On my way to Ginger's yesterday I stopped and bought her a pair of tennis shoes. Red high-tops with rainbow laces. All afternoon she couldn't take her eyes off her feet. Now I want to buy her some clothes. I want to make her dinner, give her hair a trim.

Every so often I'll put my arms around her. I do it without thinking, as if that sort of thing comes naturally to me.

Already I've begun to lose sleep over her, imagining various dangers. Where will this end? Remember the time you had strep throat and mono, and none of the antibiotics was working, and I was so worried I lost as much weight as you did?

I need an ally. I need to win over her mother.

~

Ginger's sister, Margarita, has a birth defect—some problem with her heart; she's five years old and has never been home from the hospital. "That must be hard," I remarked, "living in a hospital." Ginger thought about this a moment, then said, helpfully, "She's really good with her Etch A Sketch."

Two months of summer are gone, and still Ginger's parents haven't taken her anywhere. While you always roamed with a retinue, she spends most of her time on the curb, living inside her books. I've promised to take her to the Steinhart Aquarium—she wants to see "those turtles that know where to go."

~

I did it. I broke the ice with Ginger's mother. At first she was reluctant to open the door, but I was armed with donuts and coffee, and she couldn't very well refuse; when she found out I wanted to buy some cosmetics, she rushed me right into the kitchen.

She hauled down her sample case from atop the refrigerator and ransacked the drawers and cupboards looking for her catalog. I could see from the layer of dust on the sample box why she was so excited about the prospect of a sale. The house was cluttered but not dirty, better than I had anticipated. There was pinto shag carpeting in the living room and some chintzy orange furniture and a coffee table covered with tools and automotive parts. In the middle of the kitchen table was an ashtray in the form of a small tire, its hubcap loaded with butts. I sipped my coffee and tried to read the notes on the wall calendar, from which a basset hound in a party hat stared back at me.

Having located the catalog, Ginger's mother lit up a Kool and sat down. Parking her cigarette on the ashtray's sidewall, she raised the lid of the wooden case, revealing dozens of tiny lipsticks and tubes of cream and miniature palettes of eye shadow. Dress-up, I thought. Halloween. Referring to a brochure, she launched into a halting presentation on hypoallergenics and skin types. She was trying, I could see that, and I felt sad watching her finger, with its chipped nail polish, trace the words she was reading.

I ordered about fifty dollars' worth of merchandise, some of which I'm even going to use (the dreary stuff, like sunscreen and moisturizer). She was grinning with pride as she wrote out the receipt, and I was struck by the change in her. She's like most people,

Bett: uncomely and luckless, and eager in spite of herself. I was very pleased with the way things went, and Ginger, waiting out front, was elated.

With her father I'm getting nowhere. Not that I do much more than wave when I see him (he never waves back). I think it's worse since I befriended his wife; now he's outnumbered, forced into tolerance. The enormity of his spite disturbs me. There is guilt underneath; I'm certain of it.

~

I miss your letters. Even though I couldn't decipher some of your phrases, couldn't navigate your turns of thought, I could see you behind the words, as if I were watching you through a veil of leaves. Sometimes there'd be a clearing, and you'd emerge plain as day, and my heart would pound as I tried to follow, but then you'd slip back into the woods, to places I couldn't go.

For fourteen years we shared a room. I knew you like no one else did. It's okay that you can't remember—I remember enough for the both of us.

So now you're lying in bed. The room is damp, and the sheets smell musty, like old canvas. You are wearing the pajamas I just sent; your fingers play with the buttons. You didn't see its shadow, you didn't hear its wings, but you know an owl just passed by your window on its last run before dawn.

~

Her father said no, I couldn't take Ginger to the Steinhart Aquarium. It didn't help that I pressed him for a reason. He got mad then, told me it was none of my business, that Ginger was none of my business either, and from now on I'd better just leave her alone. He stood there glaring at me, and I knew I had him cornered. "I know what you're up to," I said, and that's when he gave himself away; that's when the fear slid into his eyes. "Get out of here," he snarled. "Get the fuck out of here."

I almost called Ginger's mother when I got home, but I knew it wouldn't do any good. You can't depend on the mothers.

It's not much of a coincidence—they do it all the time. They come right into your bedroom. You can't stop them.

I can still hear the door open and close, can still see his bathrobe on the bedpost. After me, he would go to your bed. I couldn't save you, Bett. You were younger than me, and I couldn't save you.

~

I bet Ginger's father is sitting on that orange couch right now watching television. He hasn't given me a second thought. He thinks he is safe.

Who will help me? What proof can I offer? We both know that Ginger won't say a word.

No, this is something I have to do myself, and swiftly.

Before nightfall.

# The Side Bar

They call this area The Side Bar. No video poker here, just a smooth brown horseshoe to lean on when your luck has run out. We get the non-gamblers, too, people intent on one thing: taking the edge off their day. And others who come in out of the cold desert night just to sit, shoulder to shoulder, among their own kind. It's not love they're after—it's proximity.

The stories I hear!

Lulled by the darkness, encouraged by the drink, it's not uncommon for people to unburden themselves to a bartender. They all have secrets they want to get rid of, and I'm entrusted with an awful lot of information about the people in this town. Folks depend on me, especially the ones who don't know it.

Louise, one of the hostesses, told me her trouble the first week I was here. Louise is a middle-aged woman who has spent too many hours in the sun. She used to be a looker, you can tell, but now, even through that hazelnut tan, you can see the blue veins and age spots, and all those wrinkles around her eyes make her look constantly tired, which she may very well be: Louise has her hands full with a husband

and a lover, neither of which she has any intention of giving up.

And Ronny Newcomb—he services the slot machines. Last summer, while on vacation in Napa Valley, he hit a bicyclist and killed him. It was a foggy morning, on a winding road with no shoulder, and no one blamed him, not even the family. He told me this in a rush, his eyes fixed on the ginger ale he was holding, and when he finished his story and looked up at me, I saw that the words hadn't helped: He will never get off that road. Ronny is a kind man, and smart; I wish I had known him before.

And then there's Carla—she's one of our waitresses. Carla is in love with a guy named Mark who owns the video store in town. They dated for a while, in their early twenties, until he spied greener pastures and moved on. Carla, who hasn't moved on, believes that he suffered a lapse of judgment and is still, "in his heart of hearts," in love with her. There is no evidence to support this, yet she remains convinced that he will leave the wife and children he's erroneously acquired and come back to her. She says she has "seen" it, that he'll show up on her porch one night, the moon behind him.

Carla wears a locket, a gold heart. Inside this heart is a tiny picture of Mark, taken in a photo booth when they were dating. He is innocent, grinning at the camera; he doesn't know that he is trapped, that years have passed and he is still twenty-four and being held against his will in the hollow of Carla's throat. I want to lift the curse; I want to open that awful little heart and set Mark free.

~

When I told my mother I was moving to Nevada, she was speechless—for a moment. Now, nearly two years later, she's still protesting. If I want to live in a desert, she says, why not a *living* desert? By that she means Palm Springs, where she and my father live. Well, there's no way I'm moving to Southern California, and especially not that fool's paradise, Palm Springs. What's that town made of besides swimming pools, golf courses, and bougainvillea? It's as if they'd put up decorations, then ran out of ideas.

White Horse may be drab, but at least it has integrity. Every building on Main Street began with a dream and involved untold struggles. Nothing useless lasts very long; stores sell what people need—milk and meat, cigarettes and liquor, light bulbs and Band-Aids, paperbacks and videos. If you want anything else, like artwork or X-rays, you can drive the hundred miles to Reno.

But it's not just the town I like, it's the people, the steady way they go about their lives, intent on the tasks at hand. They yearn, all right, but what they want is specific—a new truck, a cold beer, an old boyfriend. They don't know there's more to wish for, greater depths to their misery. They trust in luck. They keep their chins up.

The thing is, I'm comfortable here, and I'm not just referring to the obvious comforts, like cheap rent and no traffic. What I like most about White Horse is its lack of options. There's one hardware store, one decent market, one nice restaurant. You'd be surprised how restful life can be when you're not crowded with decisions every minute.

~

Louise is walking toward the bar. She is wearing a tight-fitting gold dress I haven't seen before, and I have to say she has a great figure for a woman her age—fifty-two? fifty-three? And she doesn't have to toil at a fitness club either (not that you can find one in this town). Louise gets her lean looks the old-fashioned way: good genes, no breakfast or lunch, and a steady supply of Virginia Slims.

"Hi," she says. "Can I have a club soda?"

"Sure." I pick up the hose and reach for a glass. Her eyes sweep the shelves behind me, and I know she wouldn't mind if I splashed some scotch in there, too, which I would if I thought I could get away with it. In a casino you never know who's watching.

"That dress is so pretty—is it new?"

"Not really." She shrugs. Most people look pleased, a little embarrassed, when they get a compliment. Not Louise. She couldn't care less. As usual, she gets right to the point.

"Meet me for lunch?" Lunch, in our case, happens at 6:00 p.m.

She wants to talk. About Ray, her lover, and Walter, her husband. We do this from time to time—discuss the difficulties involved. I have a salad and she has three or four cigarettes, and while I nod and chew she talks about the drawbacks of loving two men at once, the constant vigilance, the colliding emotions. I could make a flowchart of this affair, so familiar I've become with its perilous progress. Guilt, Louise assures me, is the worst part. "It doesn't go away—you have to learn to live with it." Which makes me think of guilt as a carpet stain, something you can cover with a chair or sofa. But I don't condemn Louise; in fact, I'm quietly cheering her on. Her life hasn't been easy—her mother drank herself to death, her brother was killed in a car wreck, and her younger sister is an agoraphobe who hasn't stepped outside her trailer in four years. Louise is no fool; she knows what this affair is costing her, and she knows that it won't end well. She's not asking for pardon or promises, only a little time in which to feel alive.

The break room, as usual, is full of smokers; many of them, cramming pleasures, are smoking cigarettes even as they eat.

Things are getting harder, she tells me. Things with Walter.

"You think he suspects something?" I ask, forking up some lettuce.

She shakes her head. "Oh, no. Nothing like that."

"Then what do you mean?"

She pauses, frowns. "Kissing."

I stop chewing and look at her. She never really thought about it before, she explains. Kissing. It was just something she and Walter did now and then, hello and good-bye, like any other couple. But lately, he wants to kiss her all the time.

"He'll stop me in the kitchen, when I'm doing laundry, and not just a peck on the cheek either. He wants the real thing." She frowns again. "He was never that way."

"And you don't want to kiss him?"

"No," she says. "I don't, and I feel awful about it." And just then she looks awful, more wretched than I've ever seen her. "I mean, I love him, you know? Why can't I kiss him?"

"How are things with Ray?" I ask.

"Fine," she says, "same as ever."

Ray is our chief electrician and the most easygoing guy I've ever met. He takes whatever moments Louise can give him. *Years* they've been carrying on, and the ardor, she assures me, has not waned. She hasn't told me where they have their trysts, but I have seen her reappear after a lunch break, her cheeks flushed, her coarse blonde hair hastily pinned, and I know that she and Ray have just gratified each other in one of the supply rooms. It's more common than you think, hotel staff having sex on the premises. Chambermaids, with access to every bed in the place, have the clear advantage.

"You know what he did?"

"Who?"

"Walter. He bought my mother a new headstone. I mentioned—I don't know, a few weeks ago—that I didn't like the one she had, that when she died it was all I could afford. So I went to the cemetery last week, and here's this new headstone. It's beautiful; it must have cost a fortune." She looks up. "He never said a word."

There's nothing to say to this, so I just nod and let her feel bad. Who knows how many more times she'll reach this miserable dead-end before Ray becomes more burden than pleasure? For sure it'll be Ray she gives up because Walter is the one who gives her shelter, and after tending bar for two years I can tell you this: People don't stay with the ones who make their knees buckle; they stay with the ones who keep them sane.

~

Most nights around 6:00 p.m., a guy who looks like a young Robert Redford comes in and politely orders a Coors Light. He never drinks more than two, and he always leaves more money than he should. I like to watch the women at the bar do a double take when they catch sight of him; some of them stare open-mouthed, their husbands right there, too. He has one of those clean square jaws you just don't see in real life, and his blond hair curls over the collar of his shirt, cowboy style. I wonder if he's ever considered modeling or acting, driving out of this town and heading to someplace where you can cash in on beauty. Here, it counts for nothing; here, it's worth less than a roll of quarters.

A few feet away are the slot machines, row after colorful row of them. Nickels, quarters, dollars—they all get fed. Every few minutes someone hits a jackpot, and lights flash, bells ring. Jackpots excite everyone. I hear those bells in my brain long after I leave the casino.

Business is never bad. Twenty-four hours a day there are people parked in front of those slots, seniors most of them, a drink in one hand, a cigarette in the other. I actually admire them. They've found something to focus on, and while they may not be the healthiest specimens, they are, in fact, alive, undaunted, doing what they want to do—and how much health do you need, anyway, to sit around and gamble? These folks had their days of glory, of beauty and vigor and lust, and now they are here, and I don't see any pity in that. Where there is betting, there is hope. Better to end your days in front of a slot machine than a TV set.

Randy, the night bartender, takes over when I leave. Ordinarily you'd call that the graveyard shift; here, it's just another block of hours, and more staff than you can imagine vie for this shift—and not just because the tips are better. That's what happens in these gambling towns. A counter-species develops, a group that prefers to move about when the world is cool and dark.

It takes a while to get used to living in a place where there are people spending money every hour of every day. You think about those people when you're lying in bed; you understand all at once that 3:00 a.m. is no different than 3:00 p.m.—it's just darker. You realize how many ways there are to live a life and what cheer these rousing casinos must bring to the lonely and the sleepless.

~

A couple months ago I tried to explain to my mother why I like tending bar, how pouring drinks has made me a better person, and she gave a barking laugh into the phone and asked me how plying people with alcohol makes me "a better person." I said it wasn't about the alcohol; it was about listening, about understanding how hungry people are for the smallest kindness. I told her about the woman with her face half ruined by some terrible accident, and what unfathomable resolve it must take for her to walk in here. To walk anywhere.

Today I meet a well-groomed woman, somewhere in her seventies, who orders a Tom Collins "with no fruit, please."

"Are the rooms nice here?" she asks.

I assure her that they are.

"Quiet?"

"Oh, yes. You won't hear any casino noise."

She nods and thanks me, and then in a soft voice that grows more and more persistent she tells me that she's never certain where to stay or what to buy, that she used to make all those decisions with her husband until he died nine years ago, and don't believe it when they tell you that time heals everything because it does not; she misses her husband more now than she did the winter he passed away.

"Do you know who C. S. Lewis is?" she says, lifting her head and looking straight into my eyes; hers are shimmering with tears.

"He was an author."

"That's right. His wife died young. He said he never knew that grief felt so much like fear." Her expression hardens as she pulls her wallet out of her purse. "He's right. You don't think you can survive it."

~

It's not just the people here who have stories—it's the land. In Elko County there's a town that was built on a blizzard-whipped mountaintop where someone found gold in the 1860s. The elevation was 10,000 feet, and nearly everything the townsfolk needed had to be hauled up the icy slopes—whiskey was cheaper than water.

Every month or so I drive to a ghost town I haven't been to before. I've walked into listing, cobwebbed shacks, found tin cups and plates still on the tables. Today I'm in Rosamund, about two hours east of White Horse. There isn't much left: stone foundations, a roofless drugstore, parts of the sagging saloon. Dealers and collectors have picked the place clean, but roughing up the dirt I find two unbroken bottles: Hamlin's Wizard Oil Liniment and SOS Vermin Killer.

While April is usually a cool month in the high desert, the temperature today is over eighty, so I hike up a stony slope and eat lunch in the scant shade of a juniper. The sky is blue, the mountains brown—just two colors taking care of everything. There is no sound: no chirping birds, no babbling brooks, no car engines, just a huge silence to slip into. I could be the last person on earth.

I take a bite of my ham sandwich and ponder the crumbling square of a house where people once ate, slept, fought, made love, had children, got sick, and died. Looking at the drugstore, I have no trouble envisioning the miners, dirty, coughing, walking in and out of the door. I conjure up an old yellow dog lying in the shade, a couple of prostitutes leaning up against the posts, laughter and piano music coming from the saloon. It doesn't take much imagination to evoke those days. Nevada has more ghosts than living people, and the land is strewn with what's left of their dreams.

It's dark by the time I get to the outskirts of White Horse, and there's a gorgeous pink line in the west, just above the black horizon. I stop the car and roll down the window, let the night air wash over my face. It smells of sage and silver, of mica and cold, clean bone. Out there, all around me, are creatures I can't see, small desperate animals darting over the rocks. What I *can* see are the neon lights of town and, even from this distance, the White Horse Casino sign: a tall, smiling cowboy holding the ace of hearts.

The coyotes are howling. They do this almost every night—launch their plaintive chorus into the starry heavens. Are they joining forces, organizing a hunt? Or do they just need to know they're not alone?

Last month a chef in Reno pricked his thumb on a contaminated chicken bone and died ten days later. A friend of mine was struck and killed by a falling eucalyptus tree while she was jogging. Take all the precautions you want—staying alive is a stroke of luck.

I think that's why I like the desert so much—all this terrifying space, this nothingness, and me just a dot in the middle of it.

Okay. Here I am. Come get me.

~

One of the managers is covering the bar when I show up for my shift. His name is Todd, and despite the air-conditioning he is sweating. He is always sweating; he weighs 300 pounds, easy. I worry about him keeling over one day. I've already seen two heart attacks in this casino.

"Watch the guy in the yellow shirt," he whispers, his big, shiny face about two inches from mine. His breath smells like onions, and I can see oil stains on his shirt, probably from "The Godfather," one of our meatiest sandwiches. "He's had four Stingers."

At least once a week I have to cut somebody off. Most of the time they're okay about it, drunk enough to be compliant. But once in a while they get ugly, and that's when I pick up the hotel phone behind the bar. Ten seconds later an eager bouncer appears, and I just give a nod toward the problem, and he or she is removed. These little scenes are actually good for business, providing no-cost entertainment and the chance to feel righteous.

Todd lumbers off, and I check my stock, making sure I have all the garnishes I need. This is the night the Bingo Girls come in. That's what they call themselves; they have it embroidered on sky-blue vests with white piping. There are six of them, all in their seventies and eighties. Every Wednesday they're here for cocktails and the fried chicken special, then they play bingo for a couple hours. Since I'm the dining room bartender until 6:00 p.m., I'm the one who gets their drink orders: two Manhattans, two gimlets, a whiskey sour, and a triple-olive martini. When there's not too much casino noise I can hear them in the dining room, shrieking and laughing, having what seems to me the time of their lives.

Ronny Newcomb, who's been working on the dollar slots, sits down at the bar. He looks bad; he's lost weight, and there's dandruff on the shoulders of his green polo shirt. I put a glass on the bar and fill it with ice and ginger ale. Ronny never orders alcohol, even when he doesn't have to drive anywhere afterward. Carla told me he used to drink gin and tonics, but after the accident he switched to ginger ale. "It's weird," she said. "He wasn't a heavy drinker, and he wasn't drunk when he hit that boy. It was in the morning; it was foggy."

I know why he doesn't drink. He's afraid of it. He doesn't believe he deserves the feeling.

"Hey, good-looking, how about making me a drink?"

I turn my head and look into the grinning face of a seven-foot man in a Stetson. He is wearing a tan suit, and his shoulders are enormous, but it's his mouth that's so startling—I don't think I've ever seen so many teeth in one mouth: big, gleaming squares, all canted forward, heading right for me.

"Your best whiskey, sweetheart. Skip the ice."

I pull down a glass, load it with Chivas, and slide it across the bar. His hand, a large flat paw, comes forward.

"Thanks darlin'. Keep it open."

Carla sprints up to the bar, tells me the Bingo Girls have arrived. Making drinks for them, the other diners, and a surprising number of Side Bar customers, I keep busy for most of my shift. The guy with the teeth is a big drinker and a loud talker, and between him and a raucous foursome, I have a hard time hearing the orders. There's one man who won't look up when I ask him what he wants, and when I lean in closer he lifts his head for a split second, and I see the reason: a ragged purple birthmark covers nearly half his face; otherwise he might be handsome. I make him a drink; that's all I can do.

~

Last night a young woman came in—I can't stop thinking about her. Her hands were shaking so badly that she kept sloshing her drink on the bar.

The blanched cheeks, the dark skin under her eyes—illness was my first guess, hers or someone she loves. Unwanted pregnancy, maybe. Or perhaps she's on the run, in deeper trouble than even a bartender can handle. I'm afraid of that moment. I know it's coming: Sooner or later, one of these customers is going to tell me something only a jury should hear.

I'll never know what was troubling this girl. Halfway through her vodka tonic she bolted, leaving a twisted napkin and a few dollar bills.

Maybe she found enough courage to go home and tell her husband she has cancer, something rare and dreadful, tumors in her brain.

Maybe he beats her and she made up her mind, right there in the bar, to leave him. Take her sleeping baby and vanish into the dark.

Maybe she'll fight back. Take a knife from the kitchen drawer, stalk him in his sleep. Maybe she'll use a gun, finish him off with his own hunting rifle.

~

The Side Bar is a disaster. The floor is sticky with spilled grenadine, and there are dirty glasses piled in the sink. What really makes me mad is the bar caddy. Everything in it has to go: the rusty lime wedges, the soggy orange rounds, the flaccid cherries, the slimy, smelly onions. Sarah, the new bartender, did this. What kind of person serves rotten food? You have to have a mean streak to care that little.

I'm swabbing up the last of the grenadine when the Bingo Girls file past the bar—five of the six. Todd sidles up and whispers that one of them had a stroke and is in the hospital, can't walk or talk. Though they are gamely dressed in their sky-blue jackets, no one is laughing, or even talking. I make eye contact with Berle, the tall one with the jewelry, and she gives me a polite nod. She is holding onto the arm of another woman, and as I watch their brave blue backs leave the room, I know they must be thinking—at least one of them must be thinking—Who is next?

~

Everyone is talking about Ronny Newcomb. He didn't show up for work last week, and this morning they found his car on a dirt road a few miles south of Winnemucca. There was no damage to the vehicle, and the gas tank was still half full.

I doubt anyone will bother retrieving Ronny's car, not with all the miles he put on it. Already it is keeping silent company with the countless other remnants out there—the spurs and picks and wagon wheels, the smelters and sheds and fallen-down fences, the cups and plates still waiting. No sign of the struggle, just the surrender.

"He just disappeared," Todd says. "Gone."

"What could've happened to him?" Louise says, frowning.

"Maybe he was abducted," Carla offers. "Remember Roswell and that flying saucer they found?"

Todd dismisses this with a wave of his chunky arm. "It's got nothing to do with spaceships. I bet he stole some money. I bet he had a buddy pick him up out there."

"He could have been murdered," Carla says. "Maybe he was in trouble. Maybe he owed someone money." Her eyes widen. "Maybe it had something to do with that boy on the bike. Revenge or something."

Of all these theories, alien abduction is probably the most likely.

I knew Ronny pretty well, and I know that money didn't matter a whit to him. And the family of that boy he killed? They wouldn't bother with revenge. They know that Ronny is already in hell.

No one is going to find him. There's no easier place to disappear than into these brown hills, and Ronny was ready.

I can tell you the rest of Ronny Newcomb's story. On a morning no different from any other, he drank some coffee, smoked a few cigarettes, drove into the desert, and gave himself up.

# Paradise

I'm tired of bracing myself for the worst. Which is one reason I left Vermont and its spiteful winters and moved to Palm Springs. You don't need pluck to live here; there aren't any hurdles. My neighbors, lulled by gratification, are kindly and placid. If a calamity occurred, they'd be as helpless as fenced cattle. It's only been four months, but already I can feel myself changing; soon I'll be just like the woman next door, who sits on her tiny patio and blissfully gazes at the pool.

They call this community West Wind Estates—the developers took some liberties there. We have the wind, all right; I just don't think you can call these flimsy condos "estates." From a distance, they look fine. It's only after you move in that you notice how the drapes catch, how the sliding screen door won't close all the way, how you can lose a fork in the gap between the orange Formica and the kitchen sink. This constant scrutinizing has brought me nothing but disappointment, and I'm determined to break myself of the habit. Everyone else has.

My refrigerator has an ice-cube maker. I am still awed by the ease of it, those perfect scallops of ice obediently spilling into my glass. Ice makers are standard equipment here; nobody knows they're a luxury.

Another marvelous device is the trash compactor; a week's worth of garbage ends up looking like a boxed lunch. Everything, in fact, is miniaturized here, even the pets: You can't own a dog over seventeen pounds. I wonder if there's a scale in the office, or one of those boxes they use to measure carry-ons. Do they spot-check? What happens to Fido if he gains a pound or two? I wouldn't mind having a pet, but I don't want one of these shivering yippers—I want a big dog, dumb and reassuring, mute as a boulder.

~

Anyone who's ever owned a parrot will know why I cherish my newfound peace and quiet. Parrots scream at dawn and dusk (ancestral behavior they can't help) and at intervals throughout the day (just for the hell of it). I can't tell you how many dreams I've been yanked out of, how much coffee or wine I've spilled on the carpet, all because of Max. And what really irked me was Kelly's insistence that we never, never startle *him*. Undue stress, she claimed, killed more pet birds than any other factor, and so we had to give a certain soft whistle—one high note, one low—every time we approached his room lest our sudden appearance disturb his reverie.

No captive bird has it better than Max. Back in Shelburne, in the farmhouse he shares with Kelly, Max has his own room, with jungle scenes painted on the walls and two large windows that give him a view of the dogwoods and the pond and the distant green mountains. He has a variety of free-standing perches to suit his rapidly shifting moods and a wire-mesh enclosure that takes up nearly a third of the room. Inside this cage are his stylish water and food bowls, several large branches from local trees, and usually four or five toys Kelly finds at yard sales. These he bites or claws beyond recognition; if he is given something he can't destroy, he shoves it into a corner. Of course, she must be careful about lead paints and glues. Captive birds are never far from peril. I learned that the first week I was there, when I heated up a pan to make an omelet and Kelly yanked it off the stove and doused it with water. Didn't I know, she scolded, that the fumes from an overly hot Teflon pan could kill a parrot *in minutes?*

It was exhausting living with that bird, meeting his needs, second-guessing his wants. Kelly said I didn't have the right attitude toward Max, which may have been true. I never did tell her what I really thought: that birds make lousy pets. Dogs and cats are pets. Everything else belongs in the sky or the water or the desert it came from. So right away I felt a little sorry for Max, even when I learned he was captive bred and able to fly, even when I told myself he was probably healthier and possibly happier living in his painted jungle, for what would he face in Guatemala but poachers and pythons and shrinking habitat? Even acknowledging their success—fourteen years of cohabitation—I couldn't help seeing Max as a bird beguiled.

Maybe he sensed my pity and resented it. Or maybe he didn't like the texture of my hair or the way I smelled. Maybe my voice vexed him. Maybe I reminded him of someone else. Whatever his reason, Max didn't like me, no matter how hard I tried to please him. You're probably thinking he was jealous, that he wanted Kelly all to himself; I thought that, too, at first. Then I noticed how he welcomed the arrival of our friends and how charmed he was by Suzanne, Kelly's former live-in girlfriend. I tried not to take it personally, but that bird was so shrewd he had me worried.

~

Some things I like about Palm Springs: the cascades of purple bougainvillea, the vapid blue skies, the easy-growing palms and the wide, forgiving streets—perfect for the large population of elderly who simply aim their Cadillacs in the direction of the market. They cheer me up, these cheeky seniors. I like to watch them rove down the aisles in their lime-green shorts and tank tops, their limbs brown as Brazil nuts. I like to look in their carts and see the scotch, cigarettes, and frozen pound cakes they live on.

Speaking of which, those freezer desserts aren't bad at all. And some of the ready-made dips and pasta sauces are terrific. This may not be news to you, but a whole world is opening up for me.

Fourteen years ago I took a job in a restaurant kitchen, figuring the knowledge I gained would enrich my life. This seemed like a sound plan, and for a while I thought it was working. I learned how to blanch broccoli and filet big silvery salmon, how to make *creme anglaise* and form bread loaves. Eventually, inevitably, I developed a palate, and that's where the trouble started. Pretty soon nothing met the standards I unwittingly imposed. Grocery shopping led to aggravation; one after another, the stores let me down. Dining out was an ongoing risk: I was offended by the vinaigrettes, insulted by the breads. Pastas were appalling, soups I avoided, and omelets were always amiss. Worst of all, I could no longer drink the wines I could afford.

The irony isn't lost on me, that my culinary education took the fun out of food. I wish I could slip into something altogether different, but having labored so long in the messy chaos of kitchens I am ruined for office work. So this is my compromise: Instead of impounding myself in another restaurant, I have joined a catering team. Much of what we offer comes out of a freezer—it doesn't need to be sublime, just pretty. We do parties, food for fun. It's a step in the right direction.

~

Kelly is a high school chemistry teacher, which is the first thing that impressed me about her (I'd been stymied by the physical sciences and had to charm and cheat my way through them). Secondly, I admired her swagger and the way she looked in pants. After that I started liking her shoes, her voice, and her ears, and before I knew it I had lost all objectivity.

We met at the Shelburne Baking Company, where she came every morning for my orange-currant scones. For three weeks we flirted at the register, until one morning she leaned so close I could smell her berry-flavored lip saver, and she said, "Would you like to meet for coffee sometime?" in that glamorous, throaty voice, and I nearly leaped over the counter. What she saw in me I'll never know, but I can tell you it wasn't just my scones she wanted. She was nuts about me, she really was.

~

I used to squeeze my own orange juice; now I can't imagine why. The premium grade in the carton is consistent and, frankly, better than homemade. Of course I buy the pulp-free variety—I loathe clutter. How anyone can eat raspberry jam with the seeds still in it is beyond me—all those little husks wedging up between your molars. Give me melon without rind, meat without bones, shrimp without shells. Life is hard; by the time the food hits the table I don't want any fight left in it.

~

Max is an Amazon parrot, and the rain forest still echoes in the deep green depths of his feathers. His head and neck are lemon yellow; crimson bands adorn his wings. The first time I saw Max I was baffled by his beauty, which seemed an aberration in the confines of the room. I could make no sense of those luscious colors, so wrong for the latitude we lived in.

They say that birds can't understand the words they use, and for most parrots this is probably true. But prodigies exist in every species, and Max is unquestionably gifted. From the beginning, Kelly said, he took our language very seriously, never uttering a word out of context or speaking out of turn. Often we had to wait a moment while he searched his memory for *le mot juste*. Most of his vocabulary was initiated by Kelly, of course, though he continually picked up words on his own and later surprised us with them. He also spoke a little Spanish, thanks to our housekeeper, Norma. "*Buenos dias*," he'd greet her, precisely imitating her inflection. That amazed me, the way he could mimic voices as well as words. Sometimes, overhearing him and Kelly, I wasn't sure who was talking.

Max also responded to dozens of Kelly's hand signals (she'd wiggle her hand, and he'd dance on his perch; she'd lower it slowly, and he'd feign sleep). This was their private language, and Kelly refused to entertain people with it; Max was a parrot, she declared, not a spectacle. She also devised cognitive tests to see if Max could discern colors and shapes. "Which one is yellow?" she would ask, pointing to a row of fruit. "Banana," he would tell her. Then she'd hold up the banana and a melon. "Which one is round, Max, the banana or the melon?" "Casaba," he'd answer, showing off.

There really was no end to the things that bird could learn. Occasionally Norma would clean our house in the evening, and Max, not to be fooled by her late appearance, would shriek, "*Buenos noches, señora!*"

The problem was, I never knew just where his comprehension left off, and as the weeks went by I was more and more aggrieved by his intellect. Could he read my thoughts, see my soul? In his company I began to grow wary, ashamed. Why didn't he like me? What truth had he uncovered?

~

    .

The woman next door—Gloria is her name—has given me a small cactus. This is not an empty gesture, for she is smitten with these squat, still lives, and her patio is a shrine to them. Obligingly I have placed it on my own patio, where it sits in a stasis between life and death. I have no idea how to help it along, and I hope it can manage without me.

There are six pools in this development, each one rimmed with flowers and supple palm trees. A wall of brown mountains serves as a backdrop. One of these pools is only fifty feet from my condo, and each morning between ten and eleven o'clock my neighbors, most of them female, open their sliders and head for the chaise lounges (they always sit in the same places). They wear sun hats and carry paperbacks and brightly colored plastic tumblers. They delight in this ritual, in each other. Their voices, coming over the perfectly trimmed lawn, soothe me.

I am a forty-two-year-old woman who doesn't exercise, and it wasn't easy, that first time, to put on a bathing suit and join the throng. Behind their sunglasses I thought they'd be judging my thighs; I imagined their mouths turning hard and smug.

I needn't have worried. They cooed and clucked over me as if I were an orphaned chick, and that very day I earned my own deck chair. These women aren't interested in the state of my thighs. They have lived for years beneath these palms; if they ever knew spite, I think they've lost even the memory of it.

~

June. Red-haired, big-mouthed June. Every time I saw her I wanted to step back, to make more room for her voice and gestures, her lipstick and nail polish. I couldn't look away, couldn't escape the force of her presence; she capsized my senses and left me bobbing in her wake.

"Oh, I *love* these accents!" she'd cry, pointing to our country keepsakes. Often she would seize an object and clutch it to her bosom: "This wash basin is *adorable*." Nothing escaped her strenuous approval. Of course, she was wild about Max, and the feeling was mutual. Parrots like flash. June's vermilion lip gloss and turquoise jacket might have reminded Max of the vibrant jungle he came from. He liked to listen to her chatter, and he spent a lot of time looking at her head, no doubt coveting that fiercely red hair.

June came into our lives suddenly. One day the drama teacher at Shelburne High got into a car accident and broke both legs, and the next day June appeared in her place. Right away, Kelly reported, she had a following—a mettlesome band of students who lingered in her classroom after school, vying for her attention. I suppose she was good at her job—it's hard for me to credit her with anything.

June was also a bird owner, which was the first reason she started showing up at our house. She had an unruly cockatoo named Carmen, and when she discovered, in the teacher's lounge, that Kelly owned a parrot, she asked for some pointers. Obligingly, Kelly began teaching her about motivation and displaced aggression and how unnatural environments create unnatural behavior. Birds don't bite in the wild, she said, and in order to stop your pet from doing so, you have to study it carefully and assess the possible provocation. June, it turned out, had been trying to pet Carmen. Stroking those soft white feathers might be fun for us, Kelly explained, but to Carmen that warm hand on her back might feel like the wide open jaws of a snake. Fascinated by this revelation, June became a disciple, and so began her long tutelage in our home. She showed up at least twice a week, often with Carmen, and they would all gather in Max's room, where Kelly demonstrated her training techniques. By the end of the first week, they moved a sofa into the room so that June could learn her lessons in comfort. Kelly advocated positive reinforcement, so instead of being punished when they were bad, the birds were rewarded when they were good. Tempted by treats and inspired by Max, Carmen stopped biting and started talking. The four of them made quite a racket some days, and, hearing their excited voices, I'd become envious. I tried to join them a couple times, but my presence only distracted the birds and, murmuring apologies, I edged myself out of the room.

June wore too much makeup. She was big and loud and self-assured. She was, in fact, everything I wasn't, and I blindly assumed there was no cause for worry.

~

Catering is not just party trays and punch bowls. We do a lot of private dinners, usually in posh homes made of glass and concrete—this sixties architecture is trendy now, and people are coming here in droves to buy whatever is left of it. Kitchens are tiny, wet bars enormous. From toy electric stoves I am expected to deliver seared salmon for twelve. While I wait for the guests to finish their libations, I like to slide open a door and step down to the pool, where the lights and flat rooftops are mirrored in the still blue water. Sometimes, in a show of solidarity, the family dog will flop down beside me. I am trembling with fatigue by this time, having worked thirteen or fourteen hours. I don't think people appreciate the scope of catering: how you have to prepare the food, then load it into a van, then unload and cook and serve it, and then wash all the dishes—all the pots and pans, all the forks and plates, and every water goblet, wineglass, coffee cup, and brandy snifter. And God forbid you should break anything.

I seem to be the only person in West Wind Estates who has a job. For the most part I live among retirees and well-off divorcees. There are also quite a few gay men here who have learned how to make money without toiling. They send faxes from their bedrooms, make phone calls from their patios, hold meetings in outdoor cafés. They are all impossibly thin. They wave when they see me, and their smiles are huge in their angular faces.

I moved to Palm Springs last December, when my life with Kelly had become a sham and a lonely Christmas seemed preferable to a tragic one. So far I have witnessed five holidays here, and each one has come and gone quietly. The stores will dutifully switch out their merchandise, and certain events will appear in the paper, but no one is bullied into participating. The modest decorations are mere suggestions—you can ignore them if you wish. That's what I like best about living here: the generosity, the thoughtfulness. There are streets in this town that have no end. Long after the shops and houses have disappeared, the streets keep on going, flat and wide and free, just in case you feel like driving.

~

Not long after I took up residence with Kelly, when I was still trying to win Max's affection, I spent five dollars on a boutique box of sesame crackers. I was trying to find a novel delicacy, food a parrot couldn't resist. The profits went toward saving the rain forest, so even if Max turned up his beak, the purchase wouldn't be in vain.

Crackers in hand, I gave the requisite whistle and entered Max's room. He was sitting on his perch near the window. As usual, he gave me a baleful look and changed position, turning his back to me. I was prepared for the snubbing and ignored it. "Hey pretty boy," I crooned. "Hey Max. Are you hungry?"

He stepped sideways, moving away from the food I was waving near his head.

"Polly want a cracker?" I asked, idiotically. Max stopped his sidestepping, and the feathers on his head went up, a reaction I mistook as interest. He cocked his head and focused an eye on the treat in my hand. Got you now, I thought. Slowly he brought the sharp gray horn of his beak to the cracker, and then he dodged it and bit my finger. I yelped and snatched my hand away; Max began preening his shoulder. He was skating on thin ice; Kelly didn't tolerate bad behavior, and he knew it. "Polly want a clubbing?" I said, glaring at him, my voice rich with menace. I was kidding, sort of, but Max, startled, stopped his preening and stared at me. For a long moment I looked into his eye, a thin brown circle around an orange iris, and, inside that, the wet bead of his pupil, the blackest point on earth, the absolute end of everything. I was doomed.

Max never bit me again (that would have upset Kelly), but he grew skillful at goading me in other ways. A good example is the time I found him gazing at a pair of male cardinals. They were sparring in the dogwood outside his window, hopping and flapping, flying off and coming back, and I wondered what Max was thinking, if he was reminded by those brilliant birds of a jungle he only knew in dreams. I pictured the rain forest, drenched and steamy, and Max, his gorgeous emerald wings spread wide, soaring among the leaves and vines. "Poor bastard," I said softly. He didn't so much as turn his head, and I assumed he didn't hear me. Later that day I learned the truth. When Kelly came home and greeted Max, instead of saying hello to her, he screamed, "Poor bastard!" He couldn't wait to get it out. Kelly looked at me aghast. Profanity, I well knew, was forbidden in Max's presence.

"Did *you* teach him that?" she demanded.

"Um, no," I said, "I didn't *teach* him … "

"Poor bastard," Max repeated. "Poor bastard!"

Kelly shook her head in disbelief. "Why would you even say such a thing?"

What defense could I offer? I could only stand there and suffer her disappointment. June had not yet entered our lives, but already I was losing ground, betraying my foibles one by one. Hearing myself talk about the restaurant, I was appalled at the trifling sameness of my anecdotes: "I asked him to prep the green beans, and he cut a whole case into half-inch dice," or, "So she told me she lost her Band-Aid—in thirty pounds of bread dough!" How entertaining could these stories be for a woman who dealt in atomic orbitals?

Nor was I proving very helpful on the home front. We lived in a house built in 1892, and all I could fix was dinner. To make matters worse, to whittle my chances even further, there was the trouble with Max. Kelly had scant patience with this complaint. Birds, she assured me, are not arbitrary creatures. If Max wasn't warming to me, it was because I was failing to understand his body language. What I needed to realize, she went on, was the importance of association. And then she told me what to do. Each morning I was to bring him sprouted sunflower seeds; I was to put them in his dish, as quietly as possible, and then leave the room. In a few days Max would learn to associate my arrival with his favorite food, and he would look forward to seeing me. It didn't seem right, having to trick her pet into liking me, but, needing his support, I did as I was told. Max, predictably, was delighted with the arrangement: I brought him his seeds, then got the hell out of his sight. There wasn't any change in our relationship, though I'm certain he lost a little more respect for me.

~

There are scores of citrus trees here, glossy and sweet-smelling, planted just to please us. From the corner of my patio I can reach out and pluck a tangerine for breakfast. We are encouraged to eat the fruit, and though everyone does we can't possibly use it all. The oranges get soft and wrinkly, the grapefruits get big and bumpy, and the gardeners tactfully dispose of them in the mornings while we sleep.

I've made another food discovery—marinated, oven-ready pork tenderloins: honey-mustard, barbecue, teriyaki, or lemon-pepper. Believe me, you can't do better. In a 400-degree oven they take eighteen minutes, just enough time for a highball. That's what they call them here—highballs. The cocktail hour is taken seriously in Palm Springs, like tea time in England, only it comes a bit later and blenders are involved.

I cut back on my catering—thirty hours a week is the most I'll relinquish. And I don't watch the news anymore; now I have an extra hour each day in which to feel good. I usually spend it at the pool with a highball. Tell me I'm wrong. I dare you.

~

Kelly and I were in trouble; I was tripping over the signs. You'd think I would have shown better judgment. You'd think, given the circumstances, I would have kept my mouth shut. I still can't explain what happened, why I steered straight into the falls.

We were dining at Katrina's, the most romantic restaurant in northern Vermont. Candlelit tables, deep red roses, discreet and clever waiters. I ordered the lobster and fava bean risotto; Kelly chose the grilled lamb with balsamic black pepper sauce. The menu alone made me want to tear my clothes off.

I think Kelly was trying to make amends that night. She hadn't been very attentive, and I know she felt bad about it. I looked at her mouth and thought about the way we used to kiss, for minutes at a time, and I thought about the day I found her standing in front of my open closet, smiling to herself. "What are you doing?" I asked.

She shrugged. "I'm looking at your shoes."

"What about them?"

"Nothing. I just like the way you have them arranged."

Like I said, she was nuts about me.

So right away I started in on the bread. Didn't she think it was stale? No, she didn't. Well, I did. And anyway I didn't care for this new peasant bread craze. Bread needed salt. And the crust was too hard—why was that supposed to be desirable?

By then she'd taken her hand away from mine and was looking around the room. I couldn't help myself: I was becoming as wretched as Max made me feel. Maybe the bird was finally getting to me; maybe he was practicing mind control from his perch thirty miles away.

Kelly said, "Doesn't the girl at the corner table have beautiful hair?"

"Yes." I nodded. "But look at the old coot she's with—yuck!"

Kelly frowned. "What does it matter?" She sighed. "Besides, he might be her father."

"Sure." I winked. "Sure he is. That's why they're hiding in the corner."

After that, I attacked the salad dressing (too acidic) and the lobster (there wasn't enough of it). I was just about to mention the slight gumminess of the risotto when Kelly broke in and thanked me for ruining both our meals.

Everything went crashing downhill after that. The next week I decided to launder the bedspread and pillow shams. I tossed them into the washer and started dicing onions for black-bean chili. A few minutes later I heard a banging noise coming from the cellar and rushed down to find smoke coming out of the washer. One of the shams had gotten stuck between the drum and the frame, causing the machine to go off-kilter. There went $400. Later that same week some pipes broke in the basement, and we lost three nice rugs and about six dozen books. Then there was the ice storm on Thanksgiving, which snapped our power lines and most of the branches in the dogwood trees. I was beginning to question the charm of Vermont. Why did anyone live on this frozen little peg? I was sick of looking at bare, broken branches. I wanted to open the curtains and behold a bevy of palm trees.

And June. I'd had a bellyful of her. She was always stopping by, she and that mouthy bird of hers. Ever since Carmen had learned to talk, you couldn't shut her up. "Good morning! Good morning! Good morning!" she'd screech, no matter what time of day (unlike Max, she had no idea what she was saying). The four of them would disappear into Max's room, and then June, that nervy wench, would sit down at our table and eat the dinner I'd labored over while she and Kelly were having their "sessions." I didn't know this at the time, of course, although I should have. It was Max who gleefully told me what was happening on that sofa.

I had come into Max's room to collect his dishes and mist his feathers. He loved that daily dousing and would accept it even from me. Seeing the mister in my hand, he opened his wings, and I sprayed him with the warm water and watched it bead up and slide down his feathers. Max rarely looked at me, let alone spoke to me, and I jumped when he said, "Love you, June."

I stopped misting.

"Love you, June," he said, louder.

What did he mean? It was Kelly's voice he was using, but I couldn't imagine Kelly prompting Max to say this. Teaching birds to utter endearments was just the sort of thing she deplored.

"Love you, June!" Max screamed.

"Shh!" I hushed. Max lowered his wings and turned around. Tilting his head, he aimed an eye at me, as if assessing my stupidity. Then, impatient, he lifted off the perch and flew over to the sofa.

"Love you, June," he insisted, hopping from one end of the sofa to the other. "Love you June, love you June, love you love you love you—" At last, exhausted, he stopped and gave me the eye. "June."

"I get it," I told him.

~

At least I was allowed a measure of dignity: A week earlier I had decided to move out, to leave Kelly and Max and all the other harsh New England realities and make a new life in California. I chose Palm Springs because it sounded like an antidote.

Under ordinary conditions I don't think Kelly would have become enamored of a woman like June. But I had proved such a poor choice that I think she was fooled into loving my opposite. I doubt they're still together, and at this point I don't care. I'm not one of those people who has to stay in touch with her exes, and apparently neither is Kelly.

Some mornings I still wake up and wonder where I am, if this place is real or just a mirage. It's not easy getting used to pleasure— there are so many things to unlearn. I spend hours studying my neighbors, noting their manners and habits.

It amazes me how well I sleep, straight through the night. And the foods I eat, the strange and wonderful foods.

I'm not fit anymore for the world I came from. The other day it occurred to me that Max and I are in the same predicament. We're both living in paradise, and neither one of us can leave.

# Acknowledgments

The author wishes to thank the editors of the following journals in which these stories appeared, in slightly different form.

"Archaeology After Dark": *Artisan*, Winter 1998 (as "Desert Night"); *Conversations Across Borders*, June 2012

"A Sea Change": *Lynx Eye*, Winter 1998; *The Summerset Review*, Sept 2011

"Greyhound": *Pleiades*, Winter 1999; *Eunoia Review*, December 2012

"The Spider in the Sink": *Artisan*, December 1999; *Read Short Fiction*, June 2011

"Waiting for Annie": *Other Voices*, Spring/Summer 1999, Vol. 11, No. 30

"Double Take" (as "The Wait"): *Potpourri*, Vol. 12, No. 2, 2000

"Paradise": *The Massachusetts Review*, Vol. XLII, No.3, Autumn 2001; *The Blue Lake Review*, November 2011

"The Side Bar": *The Summerset Review*, December 2009

"Survival Skills": *The Foundling Review*, June 2010; *Cezanne's Carrot*, September 2010; *Stepping Stones*, February 2012

"What Gretel Knows": *Damselfly Press*, January 2012

"Migration": *The Drum Literary Magazine* (audio recording), May 2012

"Waiting for Annie": *The Blue Lake Review*, June 2012

"Looks for Life": *The Summerset Review*, Fall 2012

# About the Author

Jean Ryan, a native Vermonter, lives in Napa, California.

A horticultural enthusiast and chef of many years, Jean's writing has always been her favorite pursuit. Her stories and essays have appeared in a variety of journals, including *Other Voices, Pleiades, The Summerset Review, The Massachusetts Review, The Blue Lake Review, Damselfly*, and *Earthspeak*. Nominated twice for a Pushcart Prize, she has also published a novel, *Lost Sister*.

Ashland Creek Press is an independent publisher of books with a world view. From travel narratives to eco-literature, our mission is to publish a range of books that foster an appreciation for worlds outside our own, for nature and the animal kingdom, and for the ways in which we all connect. To keep up-to-date on new and forthcoming books, subscribe to our free newsletter at www.AshlandCreekPress.com.

CPSIA information can be obtained at www.ICGtesting.com
Printed in the USA
BVOW031400170413

318398BV00001B/38/P